this boy

this

lauren myracle

WALKER
BOOKS

boy

This is a work of fiction... are either the product of... fictitiously. All statements, ... and material of any othe... entertainment purpos... accuracy or replic...

First published in Great Britain 2020 by Walker Books Ltd
87 Vauxhall Walk, London SE11 5HJ

2 4 6 8 10 9 7 5 3 1

Text © 2020 Lauren Myracle

Lyrics to "Rock With Us," p. 212: Words and Music by Yung Pinch
Copyright © 2016 Yung Pinch
International Copyright Secured. All Rights Reserved.
Used by Permission.

The right of Lauren Myracle to be identified as author of this
work has been asserted by him in accordance with the
Copyright, Designs and Patents Act 1988

This book has been typeset in Blacker Text

Printed and bound by CPI Group (UK) Ltd, Croydon CR0 4YY

British Library Cataloguing in Publication Data:
a catalogue record for this book is available from the British Library

ISBN 978-1-4063-8936-4

www.walker.co.uk

MIX
Paper from
responsible sources
FSC® C020471

**To the finest men I know:
my fathers, my sons, and my husband**

"There is a monster at

the end of this book."

– Grover

freshman year

chapter

one

My friendship with Roby Smalls began in the men's room, the two of us pissing side by side into our respective urinals. We were fourteen. We'd seen the same movie at the Co-Ed Cinema, though we hadn't seen it together – by which I mean we hadn't bought our tickets together or sat together. Yes, our eyeballs processed the images at the same time in the dark theater, but it wasn't until the movie ended and we both went on our own to the restroom with its sticky floor and flickering light and overflowing trash can that we, you know, had our special moment.

Not like that. I'm only about the ladies. Anyway, homophobia is so last century.

Roby sniffled first. Then I sniffled. Piss against porcelain, the buzzing of the fluorescent tube light, and the two of us sniffling back and forth, struggling not to cry because of how damn sad the movie had been.

It's not important which movie it was. It could have been any movie, any of a dozen movies that summer that were devastating and real and happened to be way better than I'd expected when Mom threw out the idea and I said sure, because, as she pointed out, it was a good way to escape North Carolina's sweaty August heat. Plus, popcorn.

It was *A Star Is Born*, all right?

After the third or so back-and-forth sniffle, I glanced at Roby. I gave him a quick nod, which he returned. And then we shook our dicks and washed our hands, and that was that.

It was the most authentic man-to-man conversation I'd ever had.

Two weeks later, high school started, and Roby turned up in my freshman year seminar. I didn't blurt out, "Whoa, you're the dude from the men's room. We both sniffled and tried not to cry, remember?"

He recognized me, though. I know because he gave me the same nod in class that he'd given me in the restroom. He looked sheepish, but also like he owned it, that moment we'd had. Like, *Yeah, you caught me out, but I caught you, too. Anyway – admit it – don't you think it's kind of funny?*

As Roby passed me on his way to his seat, it struck me how short he was. At the movie theater, his height hadn't registered, I guess because of all the sniffling and peeing. Also, I happen to be on the tall side. Pretty much everyone looks short to me.

But that day in Ms. Summers's classroom, I saw that Roby was shorter than all the other guys and about half the girls. Shorter than Ms. Summers. Shorter than my mom, and she's five four.

For girls, being short doesn't matter. In some cases it's probably an advantage, since it's cute when girls are tiny. For a guy, being short sucks, especially if your last name is "Smalls," as in Roby Smalls. The world played a trick on him in that regard.

Roby is pronounced so that it rhymes with *Toby*, just so you know. By the end of the period, everyone knew the name of everyone else in the class, which is called WEB, which stands for Where Everybody

Belongs. We're supposed to talk about values and ethics and happiness and stuff. It's goofy. But Ms. Summers is young and pretty, so it's not so bad. Also it's her first year of teaching, so she lets us get away with more than she should.

This one guy, Stevie Hardman, takes advantage of this by peppering our class discussions with words like *shit* and *damn*. Every so often he drops an f-bomb, to remind us that he's a wild and crazy guy.

"Stevie, let's keep this class a fuck-free zone," said Ms. Summers the first time he tested the waters.

Stevie grinned around the room and said, "Of course, Ms. S. Whatever you say, Ms. S."

Stevie's best friend, Matt, slapped Stevie's palm. Some of the girls tittered and ducked their heads.

Roby looked at me and rolled his eyes.

Such a tool, he was saying.

Don't I know it, I replied with a chin jerk, though subtly enough that no one else caught my end of the exchange.

Stevie *is* a tool. But he's a popular tool.

A month into the semester, Ms. Summers directed our attention to a dozen self-help books shelved at the back of the room. Using them as a resource, our assignment was to come up with a strategy for "leading a rewarding life," which we would present to the rest of the class. A few kids had already gone. Today was Stevie's turn.

He propped a poster on the ledge of the smart board and used a laser pointer to highlight the title of his project, which was "Don't Be a Crappy Crustacean!"

He'd been going for laughs. He got them from everyone but Roby.

He told us that in the animal kingdom, male lobsters fought other male lobsters for territory. When it became clear which lobster was going to win, the losing lobster could either surrender – and stay alive – or fight to the bitter end, and die.

According to Stevie, death was preferable to defeat. He swept his gaze across the room, graced us with a cocky smile, and said, "Why, you ask?"

"No," muttered Roby.

"Because after every fight, the lobsters' brains are chemically altered." Stevie aimed his laser at a giant lobster wearing a hand-drawn crown. "For the alpha lobster, this is great. The alpha lobster's brain is flooded with seraphim."

Ms. Summers cleared her throat. "I think you mean serotonin."

Stevie looked annoyed at having his rhythm interrupted.

"Seraphim are the highest order of God's angels," Ms. Summers explained.

"I don't believe in angels," said Stevie.

"That's fine," said Ms. Summers. "But I think you mean serotonin, which is a neurotransmitter connected with depression. People with low amounts of serotonin tend to be depressed. People with high serotonin levels, not so much."

"Yeah, that," said Stevie. "The winning lobster gets better and stronger after a win. But the loser lobster"– Stevie pointed the laser at a pathetically puny lobster with a giant *L* on his chest –"the loser lobster's brain literally melts."

"Ew!" said some people.

A girl named Gertrude Leibowitz blanched. Then she sat up straighter and lifted her chin. Gertrude terrified me. She had heavy bangs and dark eyes. She was really intense.

"That's not true," she said. "No way."

"Way," said Stevie. "The loser lobster gets depressed and stays depressed, because of not getting the flood of sero-whatever. It's called the dominance cycle. The winners stay winners, while the losers become bigger and bigger losers."

"Let's hear how your research applies to us," Ms. Summers said. "What wisdom should we take away?"

"Um, be a winner?" Stevie said. He *heh-heh*-ed. "Always succeed, and if you can't succeed, die. It's better to die than to lose."

"That's ridiculous," Gertrude said.

A soft-spoken girl named Natalia raised her hand. She didn't come across as timid, but reserved. Polite.

"Yes?" said Stevie.

"Are they all boy lobsters?" Natalia asked.

"Well, yeah," Stevie said, as if it were obvious.

"How?"

"Huh?"

Natalia frowned. "Wouldn't there have to be girl lobsters somewhere?"

"Yeah, Stevie," said other kids, catching on. "What about the girl lobsters?"

Stevie patted the air. "You want to know about the girl lobsters? I'll tell you. The alpha lobster gets *all* of them. All the girl lobsters line up and say, 'Pick me! Pick me!' because they all want to mate with him."

Stevie's buddies guffawed. Roby cradled his head in his hands.

Stevie strode to his desk, grabbed a book, and returned to the front of the room. "And I quote," he said. "'On noting the alpha male's dominance, the female lobsters shed their hard shells to become soft, vulnerable, and inviting. They fill the air with fragrant mists and offer themselves to the alpha.'"

Matt and some other guys hooted. They said things like "Yeah" and "Ooo, baby, release those fragrant mists!"

Stevie snapped the book shut. "The alpha lobster gets all the girls, and that is why being a winner at life means being a winner, period."

He bowed. Kids whistled and clapped. This set off Ernie Korda, a special needs kid. He laughed and began hitting his thigh with his fist.

Gertrude thrust her hand into the air. "So in your fantasy world, you would get *all* the girls?"

Stevie gave Gertrude a blatant up-and-down look. "Did I say that? No. What I said is that all the girls *want* the alpha male. How many he decides to claim is up to him."

"So girls are just objects to be collected?"

Stevie coughed into his first. "Not *just* collected."

"Ms. Summers!" Gertrude cried.

Stevie held up his hands. "Don't blame me. Blame biology."

"Tone it down, Stevie," Ms. Summers warned.

Roby lifted his head. "Actually, failure is more valuable than success," he said.

"Dude," Stevie said.

"Care to elaborate?" said Ms. Summers.

"We learn from failure. What do we learn from success?"

"How to keep succeeding," said Stevie.

"And it's a cop-out to say we're governed by biology," Roby said. "Once upon a time, maybe. When we were cavemen."

"And cave*women*," Gertrude interjected.

"Maybe lobsters behave according to lobster biology, but aren't humans smarter than that?" Roby shot Stevie a glance that said, *I am, anyway. As for you...?*

"Burn!" crowed Matt.

"I'm not talking about intelligence," Stevie said. "I'm talking about basic primal urges."

"*Urges*," Matt echoed. He wagged his big woolly-mammoth head.

"Shut up, Matt," Stevie ordered. He turned back to Roby. "Let's say a girl, a pretty girl, walks up to you and takes off all her—"

"That's enough," Ms. Summers said sharply. At the back of the room, Ernie had gotten pretty loud. Usually he was accompanied to his classes by an aide, but today the aide was absent.

Ms. Summers walked to his desk. "Ernie, can you calm down? Or do you need to go to the resource room?"

Ernie was a sweet kid. He loved those white powdered donuts that come in a bag, and he was always offering them around and wanting to share. But now he laughed and banged his thigh, over and over.

"Okay," Ms. Summers said, urging Ernie to his feet. She looked frazzled. "I'll be back in two minutes," she told us. "But this discussion is over. Sadie, you're up next. Be ready."

"Yep," said Sadie. She waited until Ms. Summers left the room, then pulled out her phone, stuck in earphones, and closed her eyes.

The rest of us turned back to Stevie and Roby.

"So, Roby, as I was saying: pretend a pretty girl walks up to you and takes off all her clothes," Stevie said.

"Why does she have to be pretty?" Gertrude demanded.

"Fine, any girl," Stevie said. "But if you're a guy, if you're a red-blooded American male, and a naked girl *offers* herself to you..."

Stevie had to have known that all the boys in the room were now envisioning this imaginary naked girl. It felt wrong, especially since half the kids in the class were real live girls, and beneath their clothes, they were naked as well.

Why is a naked girl so much more vulnerable than a naked guy? We guys were naked beneath our clothes, too, but it didn't mean the same thing.

"Drop it, Stevie," Roby said.

"Listen, man, you can be as politically correct as you want," Stevie said. "But at the end of the day, you've got this girl – pretty or not, I don't give a shit – and she's saying, 'Come and get it'..." He rubbed the bridge of his nose. "You're telling me you wouldn't be all over that?"

"I'm not telling you anything," Roby said.

"So that's a no?"

"Screw you."

"Bro, you're missing the point," Stevie said. "I'm not on the menu."

It was so stupid. Stevie was so stupid. But kids laughed, and Roby flushed and slid lower in his seat.

Stevie turned to Matt. "What about you, buddy?"

"Would I have sex with a naked chick?" Matt said. "Um, *duh*."

"Torin?" Stevie said.

Torin stretched his legs and crossed one foot over the other. "I mean, if the girl is willing..."

"She is."

"I'm not going to turn her down. That would be rude."

They slapped palms.

"Paul," Stevie said, "you'd say yes to free sex, right?"

Paul as in me.

"Paul, please," said Gertrude.

"Ooo, d'you hear that?" Matt said. He adopted a falsetto. "'Paul, please!' She's begging for it!"

Spots of color rose on Gertrude's cheeks.

I wondered what was taking Ms. Summers so long.

Stevie gazed at me, eyebrows raised. Sweat dampened my pits. Fear sweat. I try to come across as confident, but the truth is I'm awkward and lonely and, more often than not, I feel like a scared little kid.

"Paul?" Stevie pressed.

Saying nothing wasn't good enough. Saying nothing was like watching from a crowd as some guy got beat up and not doing a thing to help him.

So, okay, I decided. I'd tell Stevie "no."

And I would have. I swear. But Stevie was already sauntering back to his desk. He clapped me on the shoulder and said, "Good man, Paul."

"Yeah," said Matt. "Get you some!"

"You're a dick, Matt," I said.

Stevie chuckled.

I really hate it, the way certain guys chuckle.

chapter

two

I've only eaten lobster once. I've for sure never eaten it in Brevard, the North Carolina mountain town where I live with my mom.

I was born in Brevard. I've lived here all my life. But Mom grew up in Atlanta, and my grandparents live there still. They belong to a fancy country club, which is where I tried lobster, which was delicious. It was covered in crushed saltine crackers, all drenched in butter and baked to golden perfection – the tackiest white people appetizer ever, according to Mom.

I love my grandparents a lot. Granddad takes me to Waffle House every time I visit, as well as Krispy Kreme, where we pick up a dozen glazed originals to "bring back to the ladies." He has an app that lets him know when the doughnuts are ready. It's called Fresh Off the Grease.

Grandmom likes art, so she and I go to museums and art shows. I'm hoping one day she'll take me to New York. New York has a Gucci store and Louis Vuitton and a brick-and-mortar Off-White boutique. Going there would be dope.

Grandmom and Granddad spoil me because they love me, but also because I'm their only grandkid. I almost had a sister, but she died before she was born.

Her name was Willow.

Anyway, one of Granddad's favorite sayings is, "Walk into a room like you own it, and everyone will assume you do."

That's what I tried to do when I strode into the cafeteria on the day of Stevie's lobster presentation, and I guess it worked, because Stevie spotted me from his table and waved me over.

Ah, shit, I thought. It wasn't Stevie I wanted to impress. I'd hoped I was done with him, or he with me.

I told myself to be cool. I crossed the room, brown paper lunch sack in hand. Ernie Korda held out his fist as I passed, and I gave him dap.

When I reached Stevie, I said, "'Sup?"

"Sit," Stevie said.

I dropped into a chair and nodded at the others: Stevie's friend Matt and two girls, Lily and Sabrina. I upended my lunch bag, emptying its contents before me.

"Takis. Excellent," Stevie said. He snatched the green foil bag, ripped it open, and shook some into his mouth. "May I? Excellent."

"You used *excellent* twice in a row," Lily pointed out.

"Not in a row," Stevie said. "'In the same sentence family' would be more accurate."

"You should work on your adjectives," Lily said. "Variety's the spice of life."

"Mmm. Spice. I like a girl who's spicy." He dipped his hand into my bag of Takis, helping himself to more. He licked his fingers and smeared Lily's cheek with Takis spit.

"Gross," Lily said. She swiped at her cheek with her napkin.

"I marked you. Now you're mine," Stevie said.

"No."

"You have to be my sex slave and rub my feet."

"No, and again, gross," said Lily.

"Why your feet?" Sabrina asked Stevie. "Not that I'm knocking foot rubs, but of all the body parts in the world to make your sex slave rub..."

Lily shoved Sabrina. "Oh my god!"

"I'm just saying," Sabrina said.

"Girls, girls," Stevie said soothingly. "You can rub me wherever you want. My body is your playground."

Lily and Sabrina looked at each other. They giggled, and it was kind of like they *were* Stevie's sex slaves, only without any actual sex. Presumably without any actual sex.

Across the cafeteria, I spotted Roby eating his lunch and reading a paperback. He seemed fine, and I felt an irrational flare of annoyance. Here I was, feeling ashamed of myself on multiple levels,and Roby was oblivious. Roby was as happy as a clam!

Were clams and lobsters related? Did clams skulk along the ocean floor angling for fights, each hoping to be dubbed the mighty Clam King?

I imagined a clam stretching its rubbery body to its full length and flinging itself forward against its shell. Best-case scenario, the clam would drift through the water, clink shells with its opponent, and sink lazily back to the bottom of the sea.

"Yo, Paul," Stevie said. "I was telling Lily and Sabrina what happened in Ms. Summers's class. How epic it was."

"So epic," Matt said, bobbing his oversize head. Seriously, he has a really big head, and not because it's overflowing with brains. It's just a really big head.

"And while Stevie's story wasn't terrible," Lily said, "it also wasn't the most thrilling, because it wasn't about me."

"Dang, Lil," Sabrina said, "you are remarkably self-absorbed."

"It's a talent," Lily said. She pretended to yawn, which she pretended to hide with a ladylike pat of her mouth. She dropped her hand and cocked her head. "So, Paul. *You* tell us a story."

"Does it have to be about you?" I said.

"Ha," said Stevie.

"No, just entertain us," Lily said.

Was it fair for pretty girls to demand that boys entertain them? Lily and Sabrina *were* pretty, Lily in a cheerleader-peppy-white-girl sort of way and Sabrina in a black-eyeliner-Asian-vampire sort of way.

Sabrina smiled at me.

Lily propped her chin on the heel of her palm.

"Well ... see that guy over there?" I said, indicating a junior with broad linebacker shoulders.

"Thad Parker?" Lily said.

"He went to the same middle school as me," I said.

"Not entertaining," said Sabrina.

"I was a sixth-grader when he was an eighth-grader, and at the beginning of the school year he cut in front of me in the lunch line."

"Oh dear," said Lily.

"What'd you do?" Stevie asked.

"Me? I'd have beaten the crap out of him," Matt said.

"Yep," Stevie said. He drove his fist into his palm. "Whammo."

"Wow, Stevie, you are so tough and macho," Lily said, and I thought she was being sincere until I caught the wink she threw at Sabrina.

"I would have made a citizen's arrest," Sabrina said. She jabbed her Twinkie at me. "Did you make a citizen's arrest, Paul?"

I felt, for a moment, as if I'd been lifted from my body and was looking down at myself. I wondered why I was here, and what I was saying, and if I was going to do or say anything meaningful, ever.

"I pinched him," I said.

Stevie barked a laugh. "You pinched Thad Parker?"

"As hard as I could."

"And?" said Sabrina.

"He yelped. And then I yelped. And then he narrowed his eyes and came closer, and I shrank back in terror."

"You poor thing!" Sabrina said.

"But after that did he leave you alone?" Lily asked.

"He did, yeah."

Stevie cleared his throat. He liked it better when he was entertaining his sex slaves.

They weren't his sex slaves.

Nobody was anybody's sex slave.

"Yes, master?" Lily said sweetly.

"Is it time for us to rub your feet?" Sabrina said.

They giggled. Stevie looked perplexed, but launched into a speech about how Thad was a decent guy, actually, and how the two of them used to play on the same flag football team.

As for Lily and Sabrina's foot-rubbing offer, maybe Stevie took it at face value. Foot value. Maybe girls offering to rub his feet seemed normal to him.

He was, after all, the Lobster King.

For the rest of the school day, I considered the mystery of girls and boys and life and everything.

In elementary school, I didn't give much thought to girls beyond the fact that they smelled better than boys and tended to have longer hair.

In middle school, I became obsessed with girls. I looked at girls and thought about girls all the time. I discovered boob pics on Instagram. I discovered porn. I watched clip after clip of girls wearing tiny pleated schoolgirl skirts that didn't quite cover their ass cheeks, and I wondered if they sold those skirts in some special sex store somewhere since so many girls wore them. Not in real life. Zero girls wore them in real life. But on Pornhub and SpankBang and xHamster, those ass-cheek skirts were everywhere.

Now that I'm in high school, I understand more about how things work. I know, for example, that those skirts are just a costume. I also know that it's messed up how so many guys like to look at nearly naked women pretending to be schoolgirls. Guys like me. Although don't get me wrong, I'm equally interested in watching naked women simply being naked, or naked women doing naked things.

I look at porn almost every day. I feel guilty, but not enough to stop.

I look at real girls, too. Every time I see a girl in a skirt, especially a short skirt, my dick twitches. Okay, maybe not *every single time*. But ninety-nine-point-nine percent of the time, yes, especially if the girl drops something and has to bend over to pick it up. That doesn't mean I want to have sex with all of those bending-over girls, if it were even an option, which it's not.

Mom says our culture is overly obsessed with the way girls look. I get what she's saying. It would be *a lot* to be a girl and to have guys watch you whenever you dropped something and bent over to pick it up. It would be a lot to know that those same guys were forming opinions about what you looked like, what clothes you wore, and what size your different body parts were.

Unless – do girls like it when guys look at them? Some do, probably, like Lily and Sabrina. Depending on who's doing the looking.

In class, when Gertrude got upset because of the lady lobsters' fragrant mists and all that, Stevie threw up his hands and blamed biology. Is it possible he's right? Does it all boil down to differences in our sex genes or whatever?

That doesn't absolve guys of responsibility. That's not what I'm saying. But take the whole sex drive thing, and how everyone says boys have higher sex drives than girls. Is that my fault? Is it my fault that girls' clitorises – clitori? – don't twitch when they see guys bending over?

Unless they do. The clitorises.

I could ask Mom, but she'd tell me.

I could ask Dad, but he's not around. My parents got divorced when I was in elementary school, and six months later Dad moved to Greensboro.

Another biological fact is that guys, in general, are stronger than girls. That's not a good thing or a bad thing. It just is. But it's possible for guys to turn it into something bad. Because if one human – a male – can overpower another human – a female – and do whatever he wants to her...

You see where I'm going?

That's wrong. It's more than wrong. But isn't it unfair to blame *all* males for the behavior of *some* males?

When topics like mansplaining and manspreading come up in class, it feels like all the girls in the room turn and accuse me with flat eyes. I mean, sheesh.

I think about sex when I want to think about sex.

I think about sex when I don't want to think about sex.

I imagine a girl with her legs spread, and I get excited.

I kind of doubt that happens when girls imagine guys with their legs spread. I kind of doubt girls imagine guys with their legs spread, period.

Mom says it all comes down to respect.

"God wants you to appreciate the female form," she says, "just as God wants females to appreciate the male form. Or the female form, if they're attracted to women, and vice versa for males who are attracted to men."

Then, invariably, she'll say, "And, Paul, I hope you know that if you, yourself, end up falling in love with a boy–"

"I won't," I always say.

"It's unlikely, I agree. And I love you just as you are. But if you do–"

At which point I say, yes, I'm aware that she's all kinds of supportive and would be fine having a gay son, but that I'm not that son, and that as my preschool teacher taught me, you get what you get and you don't throw a fit.

Then Mom will turn brisk and remind me that

pornography isn't an accurate representation of anything, certainly not sex. That plenty of women like porn, too, and that there's nothing wrong with liking porn as long as you understand why you like it and you don't get addicted and you know without a shadow of a doubt that rape fantasies and submission fantasies are fantasies only.

"Okay, Paul?" she'll finish. "Do you understand?"

Yeah, sure. What's not to understand?

At the end of the day, we all need each other. That's what I think. Women need men, men need women, and nobody should be anyone's sex slave.

chapter

three

Our house has one main level. That's where the kitchen, TV room, and dining room are. Also on the main level is the master bedroom, which is above my bedroom, which is in the basement. I have my own bathroom in the basement, too.

When I got home from school, I went straight to the basement to drop off my backpack and take care of some personal business. After flushing the toilet, I washed my hands and looked at myself in the bathroom mirror. Clear skin, brown eyes, brown hair. My muscles don't impress, but my shoulders are broad. I went through a chubby stage in elementary school, stress eating myway through Mom and Dad's divorce, but I've slimmed down since then. No more chipmunk cheeks.

I think I'm a handsome guy – and I don't mean that in a cocky way like, *Yeah*, I *think I'm handsome, so stick that up your bunghole and scratch it*. I mean it in a legitimately uncertain way, as in, *I* think *I'm handsome, but how would I really know?*

Mom says I'm handsome.

When I say, "You're my mom, you have to say that," she says, "No. Well, maybe. But, Paul, baby, you are objectively handsome, believe me. Enjoy it. Just remember that you did nothing to earn it."

Mom means well, but the truth is that I do work for it. It's about attitude. Take the way girls look different on Instagram than they do in real life. Like, they have a face they make for selfies, right? Sometimes it's a pretty face. Sometimes it's an ugly face. If the girl is ugly in real life, but she makes a pretty face, then she looks pretty – on Insta *and* in real life. If she's pretty in real life, but she acts ugly ... well, fine. I guess she'd still be pretty, but only on the outside.

What I'm trying to say is that how you act matters more than whether or not you're "objectively" handsome or pretty. Big truth.

I leaned toward the mirror and made a face. My lips look French, according to Grandmom. She also says they look "bee-stung." So I guess my lips were stung by French bees?

I went to my room, swept a McDonald's bag and some old French fries off my unmade bed, and sprawled spread-eagle on the tangled sheets. Mom's rule is that I get to keep my room however I want as long as I keep the door shut, although supposedly I'll have to pay a cleaning fee when and if I ever move out. Like if the carpet is stained (it is) or if the walls are messed up (they are).

Mom lets my room slide because of divorce guilt, even though it's been five years since all that went down. After the divorce, Mom and I moved into a smaller house and tightened our belts, as Mom put it. We tried not to use the AC so much in the summer or the heat in winter. We canceled our cable subscription and all our streaming services except Netflix. We stopped ordering pizza from Big Mike's, which is Mom's favorite pizza place, and started ordering from Domino's, which is mine. So now all the pizza goes to me, and Mom eats yogurt and granola instead.

I rolled onto my side. I growled and flopped to my

other side. I fluffed my pillow for no reason other than sometimes it's fun to punch something, especially if it makes a satisfying *thwump-thwump* sound and can't punch back.

I wasn't drowsy.

I wasn't in the mood to jerk off.

Was I hungry? When was I *not* hungry?

I swung myself out of bed, kicking an empty Monster can out of the way. It was possible that ants were invading my room. A line of them streamed in from the window well. But live and let live, right?

Still, I grabbed a half-full cereal bowl and took it upstairs with me. Ants are gnarly.

I found Mom in the kitchen, reading a book at the table. "Hey, hey," I said, depositing my bowl in the sink. I braced myself on the back of a chair. "Wassup, little Mama?"

She put down her book and smiled. "Not much. What's up with you?"

"Your boy's hongry. Will you make me some cinnamon toast?"

"Will you put your cereal bowl in the dishwasher, instead of leaving it in the sink to rot?"

"Pew, pew!" I said, making finger guns and shooting

them at her. She spread her hands, palms up. I sighed and trudged back to the sink.

As Mom toasted the bread and melted the butter and mixed in the right proportions of cinnamon and sugar, I told her what happened in Ms. Summers's class. I started with Stevie and his stupid lobsters and ended with Roby and how he said that not every guy in the universe would go for sex with a willing and eager naked girl.

I didn't phrase it like that.

Mom placed the cinnamon toast in front of me, warm and bubbly. *Yum.*

"So?" I said. "Thoughts? Comments?"

"I don't know, Paul," she said. "It's complicated."

"What is?"

She chewed her thumbnail. "Have I told you about the time I went to the beach, when I was seven months pregnant?"

"With Dad?"

"No, with you. I was never pregnant with your dad."

"Ha ha."

"I went with Grandmom and Granddad," she said. "Your dad never liked the ocean." She sat down across from me. "I had a big belly – surprise – and for the first time in a long time, I didn't sense men looking at me when I walked by."

"Huh," I said.

"Before, I was always aware of being looked at. Guys could have held up score cards – Nine! Seven! Seven point five! – and it wouldn't have surprised me."

The thought of Mom being stared at in that way, judged just because she'd been born a girl, made me uncomfortable. Stevie's naked, willing girl flashed into my mind, only this time the "willing" part sounded worse than it had in class.

"That sounds creepy," I said. "Can I have a glass of orange juice?"

"It *was* creepy, and get it yourself. You're a big boy."

"Ouch."

"You're not a big boy?"

I tilted my head. "Mother."

She tilted *her* head. "Son."

I got myself a glass of juice. When I returned, she said, "It was a relief, not being stared at. But at the same time, I sort of missed it."

"Weird." I stuck my finger into my ear, examined what I dug out, and offered it for her to smell.

She pushed my hand away. "Paul. Ugh. Why are boys so gross?"

"Hey, you raised me."

"Not to do that."

"Oh. My bad."

She exhaled. "Sounds like Roby – Is that his name? The boy who said we don't have to be ruled by biology? – is a rare find."

I wanted to ask Mom about me. Was *I* a rare find?

But I'd left out the part of the story where I didn't stand up for Roby. Also the part about Stevie's chuckle. So I fished my phone from my pocket, pulled up "Shining" by bbno$, and hit play. I put my phone in front of my mouth and pretended it was me doing the singing.

"Uhh, hello?" I mouthed. *"Skrrr skrrr skrrr skrrr!"*

"What are you doing?" asked Mom.

I lowered the phone maybe an inch. "What do you mean? That was me, talking to you!"

"It didn't sound like you. Who's the band?"

"You mean the artist? B b no dollar sign."

She grimaced. She's not a fan of rap – *yet*.

"It means 'baby no money,'" I explained.

"Whose baby has no money?"

"Your baby, obviously." I flashed a smile. "Speaking of, have any of your customers given you any nice swag for your boy Paul?"

Before Mom and Dad got divorced, we had a housekeeper come to our house three times a week Now Mom works part-time for a housecleaning service herself. She says she likes it because she can listen to audiobooks while scrubbing other people's toilets.

Occasionally the ladies Mom works for give her stuff, like if they ordered something and it didn't fit or if they wanted the maroon Nespresso machine instead of the black one. They're all, "Here, Callie, why don't you take this?"

Last month, a lady sent Mom home with a Gucci T-shirt with a snake on it, because her son wanted the Gucci shirt with the *lion* on it. I keep hoping one of Mom's ladies will pass along a pair of sweet purple suede Jordans I've had my eyes on. I'd buy them myself, only I don't have the funds.

Mom stood up from the table. "Zero swag for my boy Paul. Alas."

"Sad day," I lamented. I stood and cranked my music.

Mom covered her ears. "Too loud, too loud!"

I turned it off. "I'm just playing with you, silly Mama."

She regarded me with exasperation. But it changed to, like, love.

"Being a human is hard work, isn't it?" she said.

"You can say that again."

"Being a human is—"

"Really, Mom? Really?"

She smiled. "Still, you're doing a fairly decent job. Keep it up."

chapter four

At Brevard High School we have blue days and white days, with different class schedules on the different days. The day after Lobster Day was a blue day, which meant I didn't have WEB with Ms. Summers, which meant I could have pretended that what was done was done and there was nothing to be gained by dwelling on it. I wasn't comfortable with leaving things like that. I didn't want to be the guy who used eye rolls and chin jerks to say that Stevie Hardman was a TOTAL TOOL, only to do an about-face and sit with said tool at lunch and laugh, or at least smile uncomfortably, at his illuminating commentary on sex slaves in post-whatever America.

I'm not good at the dialectics of social criticism. I don't know what any of those words mean, except for *social*.

Social, I'm fine with, as in *fi-i-i-ne*. My great hope is that one day in the near future, social will be fine with me – nudge, nudge, wink, wink.

Point is, I wanted to make things better. Maybe I just wanted to like myself again.

During my lunch period, I tracked down Gertrude. I found her lounging loose-limbed on the stairs outside the freshman wing, eyes closed and soaking up the sun.

"Gertrude, 'sup?" I said, sitting down beside her.

She startled. Then she scowled. "Is invasion of privacy one of your things?"

"Huh?"

"We're the only ones here for miles. You're sitting practically on top of me."

"No, I don't think so." I rubbed my nose with the knuckle of my index finger, surreptitiously dislodging a booger.

Gertrude seemed at a loss for words.

I propped my elbows on my knees, templed my

fingers, and said, "Did you hear about Ben Hartt and the xannies he supposedly brought on campus?"

"No," she said guardedly. "Xannies as in Xanax?"

"The kids who were with him said it looked like Tylenol PM, but who knows? Guess it's against the rules to bring any medication to school."

"A parent can drop off medicine with the nurse, and the nurse can administer it, as long as there's a prescription," Gertrude said.

"Ah."

"Did Ben get busted?"

"Suspended. I don't know for how long."

Gertrude shook her head. "Dumbshit."

"You said it."

We sat in silence. I bobbed my head to a pretend beat, just for something to do.

"Did you know that the average male can strangle the average female in five to fifteen seconds?" Gertrude said.

I reared back. "What?"

"The girl wouldn't necessarily die that fast, but she'd lose consciousness. If no one came to save her, and the guy kept strangling her, well..."

"Okay. That's disturbing."

Gertrude gazed at me without blinking, like a cat.

"Is there a reason you happen to know that?" I asked.

"I read a lot of crime novels."

"What if a woman tried to strangle a man?"

"What do you think? The man would throw her across the room."

"That's insane," I said. I glanced at Gertrude's neck, which was slender and pale, with a hollow beneath her throat. "But Gertrude, I would never strangle you. I wouldn't strangle anyone. But if I *were* a strangler, and I saw you, I'd say, 'No way.' You're the most intimidating girl I've ever met."

Gertrude looked surprised. "I am?"

"I've been scared of you since the first day I met you."

"Ha," she said. Her lips curved up. "I'm gay, you know."

"Oh, yeah?"

"As in, I'm into girls."

"I figured that's what you meant. You dating anyone?"

"Not at this very moment."

"All right, well, all in good time."

"Paul," she said, "why are you here?"

"As in, why do I exist?"

"Ha ha, no. Why are you here *with me*? What do you want?"

"Gertrude, Gertrude, Gertrude. You're a human. I'm a human. We're talking."

She arched her eyebrows.

"I should have said 'no' to Stevie's question," I admitted. "Yesterday, in Ms. Summers's class."

"About having sex with random naked girls?"

My face flamed.

She smiled. "Paul, are you blushing?"

"Yes. Absolutely. Very much."

"You didn't blush yesterday, when Stevie said all that."

"Oh, I did. Believe me."

"And then you sat with him at lunch. With *Stevie*."

"I wasn't in my right mind."

"Lame."

"But I'm in my right mind now, which is why I apologized."

"You apologized? How'd I miss that?"

I grabbed fistfuls of my hair and tugged. "Woman, I am sorry from the bottom of my sorry ass."

She wrinkled her nose. "Could we leave your sorry ass out of it?"

"Fair enough. Until further notice, my sorry ass is closed for business."

She leaned back on her palms. She waited, almost placidly.

My words registered, and I groaned. "Ah, man. Will I always be an idiot? Are all boys idiots, always?"

"Pretty much," Gertrude said. "But like you said, you're a human, I'm a human..." She squeezed one eye shut. "You know, you're not as vapid as I thought."

"What does *vapid* mean?"

She laughed. "Pretty much that." She winced. "Ah, boo. Here I was trying to be less bitchy."

"You're not bitchy."

She regarded me.

"You just scowl a lot, so people think you are," I explained.

"You know what my mom says? That girls – meaning me – shouldn't scowl because it makes them look ugly. Meaning me."

"What? You're not ugly."

Gertrude looked away. Her mom probably said shit like that so often that at some point she started believing it.

"Gertrude?"

"Yeah?"

"Don't let this go to your head, but you're kinda smoking hot, whether you're scowling or not. Which I can tell you since you've let me know, very clearly, that you're not interested in my sorry ass. Which is closed for business anyway."

Her cheeks turned pink. "Am I still scary?"

"Are you kidding? Gertrude, you're terrifying."

There was another person I needed to make things right with. I found him at the end of the day, in the courtyard adjacent to the pick-up lane.

"Yo, yo, Roby," I called. I jogged over and joined him. "Robicon. Robe-a-licious. The Robester."

Robe-a-licious? The *Robe*ster? Shoot me now.

"Paul," Roby said. "The Paulster. Pocket Paul." He had an impressive poker face. "Wassup?"

"I didn't mean to call you Robe-a-licious. I have problems with impulse control."

"So you *wanted* to call me Robe-a-licious? That was your impulse, which you failed to control?"

"When you say it like that..." I shook my head, laughing.

He smiled. It was a good smile, easy and open, and it pained me to know that I'd picked Stevie over him. It pained me to know that *he* knew I'd picked Stevie over him.

I cleared my throat. "Listen. The whole stupid lobster discussion yesterday, that was messed up."

"You think?" He was standing in front of a planter, a large brown cobblestone thing designed to look as if it were made from hundreds of pebbles. He leaned against it and folded his arms over his chest. "Never mind. Done and done. But want to know something?"

"Sure."

"Stevie pretends he's king of the mountain – king of the *lobsters*, my bad – but he doesn't know shit."

"How do you figure?"

Roby nodded sagely. "Girls love the short boys. Since I'm short, they can cuddle me. Or rather, they *do* cuddle me."

"When does this cuddling occur?" I asked.

"All the time." He pursed his lips. "On the sly, obviously. In the name of public safety."

"Public safety? Or public decency?"

"There's nothing decent about cuddle time," he

said. He gestured at himself with his thumbs. "Not when this guy's involved."

I didn't know if he was two-thumbing himself seriously, or if he was mocking Stevie, who for sure is a fan of "this guy" jokes.

"Did you know that Stevie once stuck a sharpener up his brother's butt?" Roby said.

"A pencil sharpener?" My asshole clenched.

"What? No, a *Sharpie*."

"I thought you said a pencil sharpener."

"No. Stevie stuck a Sharpie up his brother's butt while his brother was sleeping."

"Cap on or cap off?"

"Cap on."

"Full-fledged insertion" – I treaded carefully – "or...?"

"I think he just wedged it between Tyler's ass cheeks," Roby said. "I mean, I say 'just,' but..."

"That's crazy," I said.

"Yep." Roby pushed off from the planter and pulled his phone from his pocket. "Wanna see a picture of my bunny?"

I hadn't recovered from the pencil sharpener in the butt hole. Now I was supposed to switch gears to a bunny?

"You have a bunny?" I asked.

He looked at me like I was nuts. "A bunny? Who do you take me for?"

"Dude…"

Roby jabbed me with his elbow. "Your face. You kill me. *Lily* has a bunny, not me."

Lily as in *Lily* Lily? Stevie's (un-) (I hope) sex slave? Since when was Roby friends with Lily?

Roby lowered his phone. "I don't actually have a picture of it, but it's cute. Fluffy."

"So Lily has a picture of her rabbit, and Lily showed this picture to you?"

"No, Natalia showed it to me. She's in Ms. Summers's class with us?"

I knew who he was talking about. Natalia, who was super cute and who asked Stevie where the girl lobsters were while the boy lobsters were busy duking it out.

Forget Lily. Since when was Roby friends with Natalia?

"Lily posted a picture of her bunny on Snapchat, which Natalia saw, which Natalia showed me," Roby explained.

"Do Lily and Natalia cuddle Lily's bunny?" I asked.

"How the hell should I know?" Roby said. "You think I've got a BunnyCam?"

My dick seemed to be getting a little stiff. Frickin' BunnyCam, promising visions of cuddly Natalia.

Redirect! Redirect! I told myself. *But also, remember to find Natalia on Snapchat. Lily, too. Why not?*

"All right, well, do Lily and Natalia cuddle you? On the sly, obviously?"

"Lily doesn't," Roby said. "She's out of my league. But Natalia..." He popped an invisible collar. "Let's just say she doesn't yet, but she will."

"Of course," I said, although I had the ungenerous thought that Natalia was as much out of Roby's league as Lily. Natalia was out of both of our leagues.

I saw Mom's car turn into the parking lot. Soon she'd pull up to the building.

"So, we should hang sometime," I said, trying to sound casual. "Like, outside of school."

"Yeah?" Roby said. He grinned. "I mean, yeah. Totally."

chapter
five

Mom and I aren't poor, but our house is small and messy. Books are piled up everywhere, and the pantry is stocked with Pop-Tarts and Flamin' Hot Cheetos and half-eaten boxes of stale cereal.

Roby's house is huge, with an entryway and a wine cellar in addition to all the normal rooms. The ceilings are high, and the lighting is airy and bright. Even the air smells fancy, thanks to a "scent diffuser" with a small fan that blows out cedar-scented air.

"Do you make your bed every day?" I asked Roby the first time I went over. "You do, don't you?"

"You don't?" Roby said.

"Ha. Funny boy."

Both of Roby's parents worked. Mr. Smalls had a normal "Hi, honey, I'm back from the office!" job, while Mrs. Smalls worked from home in order to be there when Roby got out of school.

Mrs. Smalls was very much a mom-type, with brown hair and a pear-shaped body. When Roby introduced me to her, she smiled warmly and gave us a snack of Perrier and fat salted cashews. The three of us sat together in the living room, and it was weird. We had to use coasters. The sofa wasn't the sort you could wipe Cheetos dust on. I felt overly formal and couldn't find a comfortable way to sit.

Also, we weren't going to hang out with Roby's mom the whole time, were we? Nothing against moms. Just saying.

I rolled my neck and told myself to get a grip. Grandmom and Granddad's house was as nice as Roby's. Cashews were cashews—though these were some crazy amazing cashews. I couldn't get over how chubby they were.

On the coffee table sat a leather-bound photo album with Roby's name embossed on the front. "Hey, look," I said to Roby. "It's a book all about you."

Roby did a double take. "Wow. Yeah. I mean, now that you've pointed it out, it seems so obvious, but ... *wow*."

I told him with my eyes how clever he wasn't. He smirked.

"It's Roby's baby book," Mrs. Smalls said. "Would you like to see it, Paul?"

It was my turn to smirk. "It would be a pleasure and an honor."

Mrs. Smalls made Roby move so that she was between us and opened the album on her lap. "I don't know if he's mentioned it, but Roby was born two months early."

"Mom," Roby groaned.

"Well, honey, it was a scary time," she told him, all the while showing me photo after photo of tiny Roby in the NICU with wires sticking out of him. "He was in the intensive care unit for over a month."

"Paul doesn't care," Roby said.

"Of course I care," I chided. "I could look at your baby pictures all day."

I regretted the words the moment they came out. Had I just given Mrs. Smalls the opening she'd been hoping for? Again, nothing against moms, but I already had one.

Also, Baby Roby was not a cute baby. At all. His legs were so thin that Roby's mom could circle them with her thumb and forefinger, and they splayed open beneath his miniature diaper like the legs of a frog. He was tiny and wrinkled, and in every single picture he had his eyes closed and his head turned to the side. He looked like a shrunken movie star shielding himself from the paparazzi.

"He was hooked up to a mechanical ventilator, which helped him breathe because his own lungs weren't strong enough to do the job," Mrs. Smalls said. "And he was fed through a tube in his belly – see there? – although I breastfed him as well."

"*Mom,*" Roby said.

"If he'd been born fifty years ago, even twenty-five years ago, he would have died." She took Roby's chin and wiggled it. "And then we wouldn't have you with us. We couldn't have that now, could we?"

The more of Roby's baby photos I looked at, the more uncomfortable I became. Maybe it was because Roby, as an infant, was completely and utterly defenseless. Weak. I found myself thinking that Roby shouldn't reveal his weakness to me like this, and that his mom should know better, too.

But where was this "show no weakness" mentality coming from? Of course Roby as a baby was weak. *He was a baby.* What next? Was I going to mentally pit baby Roby against a big, strong claw-clacking lobster?

Mrs. Smalls closed Roby's baby album and set it on the coffee table. "When we were finally allowed to bring him home, he had to stay hooked up to an oxygen tank. The doctor called it his astronaut pack." She paused. "I think Dr. Benton wanted me to think it was fun, setting off with a tiny baby and an oxygen tank. An adventure! But it was terrifying."

"I bet," I said.

She patted my hand. "You are a sweet boy, Paul. I can tell."

"I try."

"I still have all of Roby's baby clothes, if you'd like to see?"

"And we're out," Roby said. He planted his palms on his thighs and stood up.

"Thanks for the snack, Mrs. Smalls," I said. "Maybe I can see Roby's baby clothes next time?"

"That sounds lovely," said Mrs. Smalls.

Roby shot me a look of death. I smiled sweetly, like the sweet boy I am.

I followed him to the basement, which was bigger than my entire house. Sunlight streamed in from tall windows, so it didn't feel subterranean the way lots of basements do, and unlike my pit of a room, it was spotless. Ants wouldn't stand a chance here.

At the far end of the basement was a wet bar, in the center was a pool table, and mounted on the wall was an enormous flat-screen TV. Multiple game consoles were arranged on a coffee table, and behind the coffee table was a set of gaming chairs. They were made of leather, and they tilted back with a gentle whirring sound to become recliners, complete with pop-out footrests. Cup holders were built into the arms. There were removable pillows for the headrests. Each chair had a seat warmer as well as a seat cooler, and there was a dial for adjusting lumbar support.

"*GTA 5?*" Roby asked. "Or are you more of a *Fortnite* man?"

"*Fortnite*," I said. "No, *GTA 5*. Either." I was enraptured with my chair, jabbing buttons and experimenting with different temperatures. "Roby. These chairs."

"Yeah, they're nice."

"*Nice?*" I raised my footrest higher and wiggled my toes. "I could live in one of these babies."

"You don't say."

"We should room together at college and bring these to our dorm room. No, these can *be* our college dorm rooms."

"Hey, Paul?"

"Yeah?"

He hefted his ass from his seat and farted, and I bucked and pedaled my legs.

"Dude, that is so wrong."

Roby cracked up. What he lacks in size, he makes up for in stench.

"I've changed my mind," I said, gagging. "Not rooming with you. I'm kicking you off the island, bruh."

The air cleared. Eventually. We played *GTA 5* and talked about random stuff. I reinstated him as my future roommate.

The next week, Roby came to my house and we did it all again, although we set up shop in our unfancy main-level TV room and subbed out Perrier and cashews for Coke and Flamin' Hot Cheetos. Mom caught me wiping my fingers on the sofa and exclaimed, "Paul! That is not a napkin! That is a *sofa!*"

I jumped. "You weren't supposed to see that!"

Mom introduced herself to Roby. They both said "nice to meet you" and stuff like that. Then she returned her attention to me.

"'You weren't supposed to see that'?" she said. "You're as bad as you were at three, when you'd tell me to look away so you could steal a cookie. 'Don't look, Mom! Whatever you do, don't look over here!'"

"I wanted to protect you from seeing your son do something that could make you sad. Then and now."

"You didn't want to get caught."

"Mom, please. I am a sensitive boy."

Mom gestured at the TV. "And yet you're perfectly happy to stab people and drop bombs on them and blow them up?"

On the screen, I was consumed by lava and died a fiery death.

"Do you see what you've done, Mother?" I lamented.

Roby laughed.

Mom ruffled my hair and left us to it.

chapter

six

The first weekend of summer, Mom took Roby and me to Sliding Rock, a huge boulder in the middle of a river that people like to slide down. Technically it's a waterfall, but it's more like nature's version of a Slip 'N Slide, and anyone who claims that fourteen-year-olds are too old to enjoy it is dead wrong. Sliding Rock is one of life's timeless pleasures.

Mom dropped us off in the parking lot. "I'll pick you up in two hours," she said through her rolled-down window. "Sound Gucci?"

I winced. "Ouch. Mother. Don't ever say that again."

"That I'll pick you up?"

"Yeah, no, the other bit."

"Thanks for the ride," Roby said. "And you can say 'Gucci.' It's no big deal."

"Why, thank you," Mom said. "Time for me to skirt."

"Mom," I warned.

She drew her elbows to her sides and swished them jauntily back and forth. Maybe she was seat-dancing? "I'm going skirt on out of here, whoop-whoop!"

"This is why old people shouldn't use slang," I told Roby. I started for the path that led to the falls.

"Kk, boys," Mom said. "Have fun, be safe, don't do drugs!"

"Only lollipops, and only if a nice man offers them to us!" I called over my shoulder.

Roby jogged to catch up with me. "Your mom's funny."

I grunted.

"And hot."

I side-eyed him. "Dude. Uncool."

"You mean un-Gucci?"

I punched his shoulder. He clutched his arm as if he were dying, except he was laughing.

Was Mom hot? Possibly. Probably, to an old person. She had straight blond hair, medium-longish. She wore cut-offs and tank tops, and I guess she looked good in them. But mainly, she was nice. She smiled a lot. People liked her.

Even if Mom *was* pretty, it didn't need to be said out loud.

There was a line of people waiting to slide down the rock. Some were little kids, and when it was their turn, they walked carefully to the far right side of the rock, where just a trickle of water flowed down. Then they scooted inch by inch to the bottom, squealing all the way. Everyone else chose the middle of the rock, where the water flowed medium-fast, or the far left side of the rock, where the water roared down in frothy torrents. If you took the fast track, there was a crater you had to watch out for midway down. It hurt like hell if you hit it wrong.

The girl in front of Roby and me moved up in line. She wore a red bikini, and she was already tan even though it was only June. She was our age or maybe slightly older, and she – in all the right ways – was the definition of hot.

Roby caught my eye. I gave a slight nod. *Yes, absolutely.*

The girl chose the medium-fast path, sliding down

and landing with a splash in the pool at the bottom. She came up gasping and swam swiftly to the shallow end. When she stood, water streamed over her tits, which were round and bouncy.

What is it about the bounciness of a girl's tits that makes it so hard to look away? Other things are bouncy, like water balloons. I have no problem looking away from water balloons.

The girl climbed out of the water, losing her balance a couple of times and having to right herself. She was gorgeous. Her tits were gorgeous. I imagined cupping them and jiggling them and enjoying their bounciness fully.

"Your turn, man," said a guy behind us. He jerked his chin at Roby, who in turn jerked his chin at me.

"You can go first," he offered.

"I'm good," I said.

"Go," repeated the guy behind us. Others shuffled impatiently.

"Chill, I'm going," I said. I crossed the top of the falls and stepped into the churning water. I swayed and stuck my arms out. Once I'd maneuvered myself onto my butt, I pushed against the rock with my palms and pulled with my heels until the current swept me up.

"Woo!" I yelled. "Yeah!" I flew-splashed-slid down the rock, arms flung high, and dropped hard into the deep water at the bottom. Everything went slurry and quiet. Everything was green. I kicked my legs and shot up, shaking the water from my hair.

Treading water, I pivoted back toward the falls and watched Roby pick his way across the top. He positioned himself close to where I had, but a little farther to the left.

"Roby, wait!" I cupped my hand around my mouth. "Roby! That's where the hole is! Move farther over!"

Too late. There was a collective intake of air from the crowd as Roby torpedoed into the hole, and then a chorus of moans when he ricocheted out and smacked down hard on his tailbone.

"That was rough," I said when he surfaced in the water beside me. "You okay?"

He grimaced. Then he rolled his eyes back so that only the whites were visible and stretched his mouth into an openmouthed frown. He looked like a Muppet, the skinny orange one that only says "Meep."

"I broke my ass!" he said with a heavy southern accent.

"Dude, you look deranged," I said, laughing.

"Because I broke my aaaaass!"

"You *sound* deranged."

"Ow, ow, ow, ow, ow," he said, paddling in a tight circle and possibly gripping his butt cheeks. The water was too dark to know for sure. "I should have worn water wings."

"On your ass? One per cheek?"

"Or a unicorn floaty." He shook his head. "Ooo, no. No unicorn floaty."

I deepened my voice. "Son, you've got a unicorn floaty up your ass."

He slapped a slice of water at me, then thrashed to the shallows and clambered onto a flat rock. To a toddler squatting in a nearby puddle, he mournfully said, "I broke my booty."

The little girl, who wore a bloated diaper and a shirt that said DON'T MAKE ME CALL GRANDPA! gave him a disappointed glance.

I swam over, draping my arms over the rock. "You know what I love about you, Roby?"

"I feel like this could take hours," Roby said. "But sure, go for it."

"You're not afraid of looking ridiculous," I said. "At all. In any way, shape, or form."

"I'm touched," Roby said.

"As you should be," I said, hand to heart. I was playing with him, but I meant every word. "No matter who's watching. No matter who's listening." I gestured at a nearby grandfather type who was videoing either Roby or, possibly, the toddler wearing the DON'T MAKE ME CALL GRANDPA! shirt. "No matter who happens to be recording the moment for posterity ... you, Roby Smalls, are one hundred percent fine being a total idiot."

Roby flat-eyed me. His shins were white and plastered with damp hair. His shirt clung to him in pleats.

He made his meep face and bleated, "I broke my aaaaass! I broke my aaaaass!"

I cracked up and muscled my way onto the rock. I didn't clamber, as Roby had, but exited the water the stud-boy way: a strong arm heave followed by a smooth half-twist that landed me on my butt. I nudged Roby and directed his attention to a placid stretch of the river a short distance from the waterfall, where the girl in the red bikini stood waist-deep in the water with two other girls.

Three girls, all in bikinis, all fully cute.

"We should swim over and say hi," Roby said.

"Should we?" I said. I wasn't wearing a T-shirt, just my swim trunks. I wondered if I was freakishly pale.

One of the girls had dark hair pulled into pigtails, with water dripping from the ends. She smiled, and I fell a little bit in love with her. Even if I don't know a girl, or even if I know her but don't necessarily like her, I'm all the time falling in love for brief, intense spurts.

Roby lifted his hand. "Hey there," he called in a deeper voice than normal.

The girls giggled.

"Hi," said the dark-haired girl.

"Hi-ii," said the girl in the red bikini. She stretched it into two syllables.

The third girl, tall and with braces, gave a shy wave.

I made a sweeping gesture to acknowledge the distance between us. "Can we... ?"

"It's a free river," said the girl in the red bikini.

"They want us to go over," Roby said out of the side of his mouth.

"You go, and I'll follow," I said.

"You go, and *I'll* follow."

"It was your idea."

"Oh my god, shut up."

"You shut up!"

The girl in the red bikini rolled her eyes. The other two giggled, shot us glances, and giggled some more. Girls and giggling, damn. Giggling is like breathing for them.

Giving up on us, the girl in the red bikini turned and flicked a quarter into the air. It flipped over and over, winking in the sunlight, then fell with a *ploosh* into the water.

"Kiernan, you're up," she said.

The girl with the pigtails – Kiernan – dove into the water. Several seconds later, she emerged, holding the quarter high as she dog-paddled back to her friends.

"Nice!" Roby called.

Kiernan flashed him the sort of smile older kids give younger, less important kids. It wasn't a mean smile. Just impersonal, like a "Stay Off the Grass" sign.

"I think they like us," I deadpanned.

"How could they not?" Roby flexed his arm. "These muscles aren't for show, you know."

Kiernan flicked the quarter, and the girl with braces dove after it. Kiernan and the girl in the red bikini tracked her progress and shouted encouragement.

"They're trying so hard not to stare," Roby

commented. "They're infatuated with us, clearly, but they want us to think they've completely forgotten our existence."

"They're pretty convincing," I said.

With their backs to us, the girls threw the quarter and dove for the quarter. It started to seem funny.

"We blew it, didn't we?" I said.

"I wouldn't say *we*," Roby said. "But you blew it, yeah. I'm pretty embarrassed for you."

"I'm embarrassed for myself. But maybe it's not too late."

"How do you figure?"

"Easy," I said. "I'll bow out, since I'm the fool who messed things up, and you can make your move."

"You'd do that?"

"You bet I would." I glanced at the girls. "Go on over now. Why not?"

"Why not indeed?" Roby said. "Though I do have one small tweak to the plan."

"I'm listening."

"You go first," he said. "I'll follow. For real, man, I'll be right behind you."

chapter
seven

When Roby grew so cold that his lips turned blue, we got out of the water. The bikini girls got out soon after. Roby called, "Goodbye, ladies!"

"Dude," I said, laughing. The girl with the braces glanced back at us, and I pulled myself together. I lifted my hand nonchalantly and said, "Bye!"

Mom wouldn't arrive to pick us up for another fifty minutes, so we decided to hike to another nearby waterfall. Brevard is the Land of Waterfalls, after all.

It really is. I'm not making that up. Brevard, North Carolina, is home to more than two hundred and fifty waterfalls. All along the Blue Ridge Parkway, green-and-white road signs brag about Brevard's waterfalls.

The waterfall we hiked to is called Looking Glass Falls, because one out of every five waterfalls in the world is named Looking Glass Falls. Or Bridal Veil Falls. Or either of those names in a different language.

Every summer, half a dozen teenagers die trying to climb to the top of Looking Glass Falls. The rocks are slick with moss and moisture, making them as slippery as wet glass, and yet every summer, a handful of kids attempt the climb anyway.

And then fall to their deaths.

Last summer a nineteen-year-old girl, reportedly an experienced climber, lost her footing when she was almost to the top. She clung to the side of the rock wall so tightly that her fingernails came off, and later someone found them, ten little transparent moons.

I told Roby this at the bottom of the trail. Looking Glass Falls is a serious waterfall, and I had to raise my voice to be heard. We stood twenty yards away, and we still got misted with fine drops of water.

"Paul?" Roby said. His shirt, which had dried during our hike, was growing damp again.

"Yeah?"

He pointed at the slab of bedrock, sixty feet high and drenched with spray. "You honestly think someone found ten disembodied fingernails on the side of that cliff?"

"My mom's the one who told me about it, and, yeah, she definitely mentioned the fingernails," I said. "The girl clung to the rock for three hours. She only fell when her fingernails ripped off."

"If the girl was an experienced climber, and even *she* slipped from way up there, how would someone else manage to climb up to retrieve her fingernails?" Roby pressed. "More to the point, *why* would someone climb it to retrieve her fingernails?"

"Because people are stupid?"

"I like your mom, Paul. You know I do. But when it comes to you, she is clearly all about the cautionary tales."

"I have no idea what to do with that," I said.

"She wants you to be safe, so she makes shit up."

"*Pff.* That's just silly."

"The boy who jumped off his skateboard and landed in a nest of vipers?" Roby said. "The boy who mowed the yard barefoot and cut off not one but both of his feet?"

"Are you going somewhere with this?"

Roby folded his arms over his chest. "The boy who

was stomped on by a giant roly-poly in the dead of night, after the boy killed one of the giant roly-poly's tiny relatives?"

"I feel like you're confusing me with someone else," I said. "I've never in my life killed a roly-poly, except that one time. After which I learned my lesson."

"Well, in *that* case," Roby said, laughing.

I heard footfalls behind us, the steady rhythm of joggers.

"Coming through," a guy called.

"'Sup," I said, stepping aside as two guys passed. The first guy flicked his eyes at me for a millisecond. Neither responded.

Roby and I watched them go. They wore shoes, socks, and tiny running shorts. No shirts. They were fit in that crazy way that certain people who aren't me sometimes are, people who do push-ups for fun and compete in triathlons on their days off. Or run up mountains.

"Can we deduct points for their shorts?" Roby asked in a low voice.

"We have to," I said. "We have no choice."

We sighed.

"I'm going to start working out," Roby said. "Tomorrow. Or if not tomorrow, the next day."

"A man with a plan. Nice."

"We have a family gym membership at the country club, and my dad's always bugging me to take advantage of it. Not that he goes himself." He shrugged. "He has to travel a lot for work, so."

The mention of his dad's job reminded me of something. "Do you really want to be an astrophysicist?" I asked.

"What? Why would I want to be an astrophysicist?"

"I have no idea. That's what you said in Ms. Summers's class."

He looked at me suspiciously.

"It was at the beginning of the year?" I said. "We went around in a circle and everyone shared their 'career goals'?"

"*Ohhh,*" Roby said. "Did Stevie Hardman say he was going to be a Formula Forty-Four race car driver?"

"Formula Forty-Four is cough syrup. But he said he wanted to be a Formula *One* race car driver, yeah."

"Well, then, whatever I said was to make Stevie's choice sound dumb." He ran his thumb over his upper lip. "I wouldn't have said astrophysicist, though. Do you know how long I'd have to go to school to be an astrophysicist?"

"Then what do you want to do?"

He propped his hands on the wooden railing of the observation deck. "Not be an astrophysicist."

I laughed.

"And not wear ridiculously small running shorts. Or run. Unless I'm being chased."

"Fair enough."

He put his elbows on the railing, his back to the falls. "You?"

"If Formula One racing doesn't pan out?"

"Yes, if by some unholy luck Formula One racing doesn't pan out."

"No clue," I said. "Go to college? Meet girls?" I bobbed my head from side to side. "I wouldn't mind being a rapper."

"Being a rapper would be dank. Or a music producer."

"Or a rapper *and* a music producer."

"Sweet," Roby said.

"You can be a rapper-slash–music producer, too," I offered. "We could still go to college, since our rap careers might not explode immediately. But since we'll be roommates, we'll have fun regardless."

"Tons o'," Roby said.

I envisioned us in a tricked-out dorm room: shag carpet, a disco ball, one of those beds that drops down from the wall. *Soo-prise!* A lava lamp. Or not. We could finesse the details after finalizing our color scheme and shit.

We'd bring Roby's remote-control leather recliners for sure. A keyboard, a midi, whatever software we'd need for making beats. A dope sound system with woofers for driving the *womp-womp* of the bass. Insulated walls to muffle the *womp-womp* of the bass. Only, could you have insulated walls in a dorm room?

"Maybe we should live off-campus so we can bump whenever we want," I suggested.

"With no one telling us to turn down our goddamn music," Roby said.

"We could buy a pool table," I said. I was getting excited. "And a mini fridge, for hosting parties."

"A full-size fridge if we get an apartment," said Roby.

"A tiger," I said. I staggered at my brilliance. "Dude. A tiger? Yeah? *Yeah?*"

Roby looked at me like I was crazy. "Obviously."

We bumped knuckles to seal the deal.

chapter

eight

Sometimes my thoughts skip from topic to topic until – *boom* – they snag on Mom and Dad and their divorce, and suddenly I feel deflated. Whenever this happens, and I mean every single time, it catches me by surprise.

Like tonight, after having big fun with Roby at Sliding Rock and getting sunburned and tossing stupid remarks back and forth but not caring because that was the kind of day it was. Sunshine and blue skies and cold nuts – good stuff, right?

So why, after dropping Roby off and retreating to my room, did I fall into one of my melancholy moods?

Maybe it was a balancing of the scales, a reminder from the world that *Yeah, sure, kid, sometimes you get sunshine and smiles, but just remember: Every time the sun shines, storm clouds are brewing, eager to blot out the light.*

But that's stupid. The world doesn't revolve around me, not when it comes to good things *or* bad things. It just seems like it does.

If you've never fallen randomly into a melancholy mood, here's what it's like: Imagine being a little kid, and you're at a birthday party, and there's cake and games and friends, and maybe balloon animals or a magician. Yay!

Only this isn't a real birthday party, or a remembered birthday party, or a birthday party you saw on some show. This is a fantasy birthday party, and out of nowhere the lights shut off, the balloon animals pop, and your friends disappear. You have no idea where they went, or why.

You're utterly alone.

You're terrified.

Then you bolt upright in your bed, slick with sweat. The party? It was a dream party. A bad dream party. You're not a little kid anymore, but you still sprint to your parents' room, only the mounds beneath their covers ... those lumpen shapes...

No. Those are your parents, not gorillas. *Pull it together, kid.*

Except there aren't two lumps. There's just one. There's no dad to say, "Aw, buddy" and hug you and make everything better. Just one parent groggily rubbing her eyes, asking what's wrong. Just your mom, since that's who you live with now, ever since your dad moved to Greenville and started a new life.

Anyway.

When I was still little, when Dad still tucked me in at night, I liked to pull his beard. One night after I gave it a tug, he said, "You know, Paul, when you grow up, you'll have a beard."

"No," I told him. "When I grow up, I'm going to be a community helper." That's what I called police officers and ambulance drivers and firefighters back then. "Either a community helper or a lady."

"You can't grow up to be a lady, because you have a penis," Dad said. "And one day, you'll grow hair on your face, like me."

"No, Dad," I insisted. "I might be a lady or I might not. You never know about me."

Mom and Dad used to love telling that story. When they did, I felt safe, as if I were exactly where I was supposed to be. I felt cherished.

Things change. People change. Parents don't always keep their promises, I get it.

When I got home from Sliding Rock, I'd grabbed a banana from the wooden bowl on the kitchen counter even though it was greener than I like my bananas to be. Now I peeled it to the halfway mark, and sure enough, the banana part didn't have the good banana smell and the peel wasn't properly floppy.

I chucked it into the hall.

Ah, shit. I stood up from my bed, scooped the banana from the floor, and chucked it into my bathroom trash can.

Everything about Mom and Dad and the way things used to be, that's over and done with. But thinking about it still hurts, like an old bruise you forget about until you bump it. Also, Greenville's only an hour and a half from Brevard. It hurts my feelings that Dad doesn't visit more often.

After *The Talk,* after Mom and Dad hugged me and told me they'd always love me and that they'd always be my parents even if they were no longer married,

I spotted Mom in the backyard. She had on her UNC sweatshirt, her arms wrapped around her ribs. There was snow on the ground.

"Aren't you cold?" I asked, after I'd gone outside and stood behind her for a while.

"Oh!" she said, startled. "No, I'm fine." She gave me a sidelong glance. "What about you, baby? Are you okay? Dumb question, I know, but...?"

She had to be cold, even if she didn't admit it. I had on wool socks, a winter coat, and my Pokémon beanie, and the winter air still snuck in and made me shiver.

I mimicked her stance, planting my feet wide and folding my arms over my chest. We gazed at the yard. Every so often, Mom gave me searching looks.

"I know you and Dad said it was a mutual decision," I said. "And that adult problems are for adults, or whatever." I kicked at the snow and uncovered a clump of dog shit, which was whack. We didn't even have a dog. "But can you just tell me why?"

"Oh, Paul."

Tears burned my eyes. By the end of fourth grade, I'd heard enough "Oh, Paul"s to last a lifetime.

Mom filled her cheeks with air, then let it out in a *whoosh*. She said, "I realized I wasn't singing anymore."

I frowned.

"You know how much I like to sing, right?" she asked.

"I guess," I said. "But only songs about death."

Maybe it was a southern thing, or maybe Mom was just morbid, or maybe Roby was right about Mom's fondness for cautionary tales. Maybe she sang me grisly songs on purpose, to discourage me from swallowing flies or approaching random boa constrictors. But, truth, the songs she sang leaned hard on tragic.

Mom's lips twitched. "Now, Paul. What about the song about the little white duck, swimming in the water?"

"The duck who gets eaten by the little red snake? That duck?"

"It was the little black bug that got eaten, not the duck."

I lifted my eyebrows.

"What about 'I've Been Working on the Railroad'?" Mom slipped her arm around me and tried to make me sway. *"I've been working on the railroad, all the livelong day!* Where's the death in that one? All the *livelong* day?"

I grunted.

We stood there. After a second, Mom rested her head on my shoulder. At ten years old, I was already tall enough for her to do that.

"I wish I could explain it better," she said, "but that's the best answer I've got."

Best answer to what? I thought. Then, *Oh yeah, the stupid divorce.*

"You'll sing again," I said lamely.

"Of course I will." She squeezed my waist. "And guess what?"

"What?"

"I just did."

chapter
nine

At the end of summer break, Roby made a confession. We were at his house. It was late. We lay in separate twin beds in the dark.

"Do you know what I heard my mom say to one of her friends?" Roby asked. "She said that she suspected I wouldn't date until college."

"Ouch," I said. "Does she know you heard?"

"No, but screw that. My mom doesn't get to tell me who I am."

"No way," I agreed. But Roby's mom was a nice lady. She wouldn't chop at Roby's ego on purpose. Maybe she wanted to protect Roby from being disappointed, like if in the future he got up the nerve to ask a girl out, and the girl rebuffed him.

"Then I started thinking about Stevie and the lobsters," Roby said. "You remember Stevie and the lobsters?"

"Of course." I considered. "You know, that's not a bad name for a band. No, I take it back. It's a horrible name for a band."

"I looked up everything Stevie said, and it's true," Roby said. "How the alpha lobster grows bigger and more successful each time he defeats another lobster, and how the loser lobsters shrink and grow more and more depressed? Stevie wasn't making that shit up."

"Yeah, but," I protested, "is depression really a problem in the lobster community? I'm thinking no."

"It's not just true for lobsters, either," Roby went on. "It's true for fish, for monkeys, for orangutans, and – and – for humans. Male humans, anyway. And get this. Their testes get bigger."

"Huh?"

"Their balls. When one guy beats another guy in a fight, the winner's testosterone spikes and his balls get bigger."

"That can't be true."

"It is."

"That's insane," I said, first wondering what guys I could provoke into a fight, and then remembering that, oh yeah, it would have to be guys I could defeat, not guys who might defeat me.

"There's more," Roby said. "When guys have sex, that makes their testosterone spike, too. Scientists think it's because sex counts as a 'win,' just like winning a fight."

I felt uneasy. "Do girls know about this?"

"How should I know?"

"I think they'd be pissed. Or does sex count as a 'win' for them, too?"

"Paul, what if I never have sex?"

"No," I said briskly. "Not going to happen."

"Exactly, that's what I'm afraid of."

"You know that's not what I mean."

"Yeah, but do *you* know what *I* mean?" he asked. "You, Paul, you're funny. You're tall. Girls like you."

"Says who?"

"But me? I'm going to die a virgin."

It's strange how being in the dark makes it easier to say things.

"Zip it," I commanded. "No virgins will be dying under my watch, understood?"

He made an inarticulate sound.

"Under*stood*?"

"Eh."

"Roby, listen," I said. "You're a dick and a cheesehead and a donkeyboy, but you're a kind boy. You've got a good heart."

"Thanks," Roby said.

"I mean it."

"Yeah, all right."

Things got quiet. Roby's breathing changed.

I punched my pillow and rolled to my side. I hadn't confided this to Roby, and I doubted I needed to, but I thought about sex all the time. Sex, sex, sexsexsexsex. SEX!

I counted sex as a win. In theory. I was a-okay with theoretical sex. I was a-okay with real sex, whenever in the future real sex became an option. In reality, however, I suspected I was nearly as inexperienced as Roby.

I should have told him that. Why didn't I tell him that?

In my whole life, I've kissed one girl. It happened on my elementary-school playground. Just lips, no tongues, and that night the girl called to tell me she was too young for kissing, her mom said she wasn't allowed, and that she'd be in big trouble if she did it again. She said she hoped I'd understand.

I did understand. My mom, too, had told me that if there was ever something I felt uncomfortable with, some "peer pressure" sort of thing I didn't want to do, I could blame her in order to get out of doing it.

Roby would have laughed. *I* would have laughed. And he would have felt better knowing he wasn't alone in his virginal state.

I'd tell him the next time the subject came up. I'd tell him I meant it about not dying a virgin, not him or me. We'd be each other's wingmen. That's what best friends were for.

chapter

ten

Roby and I pledged to rebrand ourselves before the start of sophomore year. Roby started sagging his pants, allowing the waistband to ride below his butt cheeks. He took to wearing extra-large sweatshirts, even on hot days. He started growing out his hair. I decided to grow mine out, too, but it was his idea first. Credit where credit's due.

I'd had a head start on my rebranding, as I'd bought a bike at Recycled Cycles at the beginning of the summer to make it easier to get to Roby's house. His subdivision was four miles from my house, so on days I didn't sleep over, that meant eight miles round-trip. On days I did sleep over, it still meant eight miles round-trip. Just, the trip extended over two days.

In June, I had no muscle tone. By the end of August, I had quads of steel. Plus, I'd grown an inch taller.

I thought hard about what image I wanted to project as a tenth grader. I used my birthday money, as well as what I earned mowing people's lawns, on a few select articles of swag. I discovered joggers. I pierced my ears. I purchased a sweet stainless-steel chain.

Mom bought me my first bucket hat, a red Supreme one with a box logo that said *Comme des Garçons*. She said she couldn't believe she was spending a hundred and fifty dollars on a hat, and that I better take care of it.

I was all, "Ma. Of course."

Every day leading up to the first day of school, I checked out my reflection in my bathroom mirror. Sometimes I dropped my pants and checked out my dick, especially when I was hard. Sometimes I got hard just thinking about getting hard. I had a man's dick at last, I was pretty sure.

I was fit. I was tan. I had unkempt surfer-boy hair streaked by the sun.

I was six feet one, and my erect penis was nearly six inches long.

I was living the dream.

sophomore year

chapter

eleven

On the first day of the new semester, Roby and I met in front of the high school so we could walk in together. I wore my Supreme bucket hat. Roby wore an Empyre sweatshirt with a Day of the Dead skull on it.

We pushed through the doors and strode down the hall in slow-mo. Bass-heavy rap dominated our imaginary soundtrack. Think ScHoolboy Q or 2 Chainz. Roby's hair bounced as he walked, except "bounced" sounds girlie, so let's say his hair rose and fell in a manly way. As for me, I towered above everyone, my arms swinging by my sides. I lifted my chin and tried to radiate confidence. I was so much more mature than I'd been as a freshman. I wanted it to show.

Yeah-uh.

I was taking a photography elective, and Gertrude Leibowitz was in my class.

"Yo, Gertrude," I said. She'd either cut her bangs or grown them out, I wasn't sure which. It made her eyes pop. "Looking sharp."

"Hey, Paul," she said. "Good summer?"

She told me she'd spent a month in Venice Beach and had gotten into rap. I told her rap was dank. We claimed seats at the same table and exchanged Spotify usernames so we could check out each other's playlists.

Lunch was epic. The freshmen were afraid of me, whereas I wasn't afraid of anyone. I saw Stevie Hardman in line, and we did the whole "Wassup, how was your summer?" thing. His buzz cut looked stupid, his hair short and slicked to his scalp with product. I saw Lily and Sabrina, Stevie's sex slaves, and they were nicer than I remembered. They chatted with me like we were friends, so I ran with it. Also, I changed their status from "sex slaves" to "regular people." "And how's your bunny?" I asked Lily.

Lily furrowed her brow. "My bunny? Fine. Cute. Smelly. How'd you know I had a bunny?"

"Oh, the typical channels," I said casually.

Lily and Sabrina shared a glance.

"Which channels would those be?" asked Sabrina.

"I'm not sure how you expect me to explain it to you if you don't already know," I said.

"Huh?"

"Exactly."

"Okay, weirdo," Lily said, and she said it fondly, I swear to Bob. "See ya around."

"Bye!" echoed Sabrina.

It was a good day, which turned into a good week, and then a good month. I was becoming a more fleshed-out version of myself, and I liked it. Better at joking around with the guys I had class with. Better at catching the eyes of pretty tenth-grade girls, as well as the eyes of the bitties, which was what this guy Monty called the freshman girls.

The bitties were shiny, skinny, and skittish. They giggled when they looked at me, and when I smiled at them, their cheeks turned red.

chapter
twelve

Roby and I contrived to hang out nearly every day, more often than not at his house. Though it pains me as a lover of cheese puffs and Hostess Cupcakes to admit it, the Smalls had better food. Roby's mom kept white truffle dip in the refrigerator, and it wasn't reserved for her and Roby's dad. Roby and I were welcome to dive in, too, and we did.

Oh, and drunken goat cheese. Sophomore year was the year I discovered drunken goat cheese. That stuff's the rizzle-dizzle.

One day in early October, Roby and I were filling our hungry-boy stomachs in his kitchen while shooting the breeze with his mom, who was always super kind about asking how school had been, what we thought of our teachers, and had we eaten anything real for lunch or had we filled up on vending machine crap. The regular questions grown-ups liked to ask, but Mrs. Smalls wasn't just making the right noises while tuning us out. She genuinely cared.

I heard the *thunk-yank* of the back door opening – the handle mechanism was funky and required a special touch – and Natalia Gutierrez bounded into the house. Natalia who'd been in Ms. Summers's class with me and Roby last year. Natalia who was Lily's friend and who showed Roby Lily's bunny and who, according to Roby, hadn't cuddled him yet but would.

I'd wondered, at the time, what the deal was between Roby and Natalia. They obviously had some sort of relationship if she was showing him pictures on her phone. But I'd forgotten to ever ask.

Natalia held a steel pan with a spring on the side. She moved to hand it to Mrs. Smalls, but drew up short when she saw me. "Paul? Hi. I didn't know you were here."

"I didn't know you were here, either," I said. I shook my head. "Wait. Why *are* you?"

"I live down the street," she said.

I looked at Roby and thought, *Dude, you've been holding out on me.*

"This is like my second home," Natalia said. She placed the pan on the island and pointedly cleared her throat. "Thanks a lot for never mentioning me, Roby."

"In elementary school, maybe it was your second home," Roby said. "Even in sixth grade. Maybe. But then you got busy being a girl or whatever, so ... so..." His face became increasingly flushed. "So thanks a lot to *you*, Natalia."

"Ooo, harsh comeback, big man."

"Blah, blah, blah," Roby retorted, and for a second I could see it, Roby and Natalia being buddies and bouncing back and forth between each other's houses.

"Children," Mrs. Smalls scolded.

"Sorry, Mrs. Smalls," Natalia said contritely.

"Mom," complained Roby.

They'd gone back to an earlier time, leaving me behind.

Roby sat up straighter on his barstool, as if remembering he was in high school and no longer some punk ten-year-old. "Paul has spent hours upon hours here, ever since we became like this in Ms. Summers's

WEB class." He crossed his first two fingers and held them up.

Natalia looked at Roby strangely. I looked at Natalia and shrugged.

"If you'd come by when Paul was here, then you'd have seen him and he'd have seen you," he continued. "Okay, Natalia? So enough with, 'Oh, Roby, I can't believe you didn't even mention my existence.'"

"He did mention your existence," I contributed. "He just left out the neighbor part."

Natalia fought not to smile, but her lips curved up despite herself. Damn, she was fine.

Mrs. Smalls picked up the odd-looking pan. "How'd your mom's cheesecake turn out?"

"Really good," Natalia said.

Mrs. Smalls put the pan in a low cupboard, stood, and brushed her hands on her thighs. "I'm so glad," she said. "I'll leave you kids to it. Help yourselves to anything, just no snacks after five."

"Yes, Mom," Roby said, rolling his eyes.

Natalia came over and perched on the barstool next to mine. I could feel the heat radiating from her skin.

"So," I said. "You're Roby's neighbor."

"Way to state the obvious," Roby said. He shot me a

hard look, like I'd said or done something wrong, not just dumb. Then the look was gone, and maybe it hadn't been there at all, except I'm pretty sure it had.

It was nice outside, so we went to Roby's garage and equipped ourselves with a longboard, a skateboard, and a beater bike with a low seat and high, wide handles. Roby took the bike. As he pedaled in circles around his driveway, he looked like a miniature gang lord. Natalia claimed the longboard, insisting that was the only kind of board she could ride, and I took the skateboard.

"Bike trail near the tunnel?" Roby asked Natalia.

She pushed off on her board and said, "Yeah!"

He nodded and hung a right out of his driveway. I brought up the rear, my quads flexing. The skateboard wheels whirred in rhythm with my strokes: *THUNK, clack, clack, clack. THUNK, clack, clack, clack.* They whined every time I took a turn. The bearings needed to be cleaned.

Natalia, a couple of yards in front of me, looked lit. She wore jeans, a soft blue button-down with short sleeves, and low-top black Chuck Taylors. Her stance on the longboard was relaxed. She rode goofy-footed, her left foot on the back of the board instead of her right. I wondered if she was left-handed, too.

Girls who skateboard are either weird or cool. The ones who are weird are easy to spot. They take on the skate mentality really hard, dropping terms like "gnarly" and "railside" and "ripper" into every sentence. They smoke, and they let eighth-graders use their vapes, which is uncool for many reasons. You need to have morals. Kids that age don't even know what anything is yet. Worst of all, the uncool skater girls wear Palace merch and possibly own Palace skateboards, but they look so stupid, they degrade the Palace brand.

The cool skateboarding girls, on the other hand, are chill. That's really it. If they're pretty, like Natalia, that's icing on the cake.

Roby looped and swerved on his bike in order to not get too far ahead. We talked about Ms. Summers, since she was something we all had in common, arguing about whether she qualified as a hipster or a hippie.

"Hipster, because she wears vests and funky jewelry," I said.

"Yeah, hipster," said Roby. "She gave everyone mustache stickers that one day, remember?"

"Nope, hippie," said Natalia. She smiled triumphantly. "She uses a crystal deodorant. She keeps it in her top desk drawer."

I groaned.

"How do you know that?" Roby said.

"I know everything," Natalia said.

"Have you checked this year?" he challenged. "Maybe she switched to real deodorant."

"Give it up, Roby," she said. "I'm right. You're wrong."

"Yeah, Roby," I said.

Once we reached the bike trail, there were ridges in the asphalt at even intervals. Each time I crossed one, my skateboard jumped. The section of trail we were on was flat, but ahead of us was a savage hill where the trail banked steeply down and disappeared into the mouth of a tunnel.

Natalia swung her left foot down and pushed. Roby stopped holding back and let himself fly, hunching forward over the handlebars for less wind resistance. I felt a flutter of fear and braced my core.

"Yeah!" Natalia cried as she picked up speed.

"Wooooo!" responded Roby.

Wind in our hair, sun on our skin, school done for the day and stored safely on a shelf until tomorrow ... damn, this being alive thing felt frickin awesome.

Then Natalia's posture changed. It happened too quickly to pinpoint how or why. Her arms flailed, and she leapt from her board. She took two lurching strides forward before going down hard. Her palms slapped the asphalt, but her knees bore the brunt of her fall.

I jumped off my skateboard, kicking it toward the grass alongside the trail and racing for Natalia. "Roby, hold up!" I called. "Natalia's hurt!"

"Ow," Natalia said, rocking back and forth. "Ow, ow, ow." She said it as if it were funny, as if she were embarrassed and making light of her spill. I knelt beside her and winced. Her jeans were ripped, and the flesh below was torn and sticky with blood.

Natalia smiled for one more second before her chin trembled and her mouth tugged downward. Then she was crying instead of laughing, while continuing to rock and say "ow."

"At first I didn't think it was that bad," she said through her tears. "I thought, 'Oh, bummer, but at least I didn't hurt myself.'"

Roby skidded to a stop in front of us. He joined me at Natalia's side, his expression worried. "What happened?"

"I got going too fast, so I bailed," Natalia said.

"Can you stand? Can you walk?" he asked. There

were tiny rocks embedded in her cuts. "Let's get you home."

Natalia slung one arm around me and the other around Roby, and we helped her limp up the hill. We left the skateboards and the bike behind. It was a safe neighborhood. No one would take them.

"I am such an idiot," she said.

"No," said Roby.

"Everyone falls," I said. "It happens."

She laugh-cried. Her eyes were glossy, and her lashes were wet and long. "Ouch," she said. She hopped on her right foot, bearing down harder on us, then stopped. "Guys. Sorry. I just—"

"I'll call my mom," Roby said. He reached for his phone, throwing Natalia off-balance. She wobbled, but I caught her.

I scooped her into my arms, because I could.

She laughed and held on to my neck.

"Dude—" Roby started.

"No worries, I've got it," I said.

"I'm not too heavy?" Natalia asked.

She was not too heavy. She was perfect. She smelled amazing, and I wondered what kind of soap she used. Then I wondered if she took baths or showers, because, you know, soap. Then I snapped out of it and planted one foot in front of the other, again and again, until we reached Natalia's house.

It wasn't that far. Still, Roby wouldn't have been able to carry her all that way. I knew it and he knew it, and probably Natalia did, too.

But Natalia was bleeding. She was in pain. I was like a firefighter, carrying her to safety.

Natalia's mom fussed and cooed over Natalia's wounds, then fussed and cooed over me and Roby.

"Lena, get these boys a Coke," she told Natalia's sister. Lena was nine years old, in the fourth grade, and loved reading, unicorns, dolphins, and narwhals, as she enthusiastically told me. She was super cute and super chatty.

"Okay," Lena said finally, running off.

"Such good boys," Mrs. Gutierrez said. "Thank you for taking care of my Natalia."

Lena reappeared with a notepad and a pencil. "I'm ready to take your orders," she said. "What would you like?"

"Lena!" Natalia exclaimed.

"I'll take a Coke, please," Roby said.

"Do you have any chips?" I said.

"Paul!" exclaimed Roby.

"What?" I understood how little kids worked. If Lena wanted to be a waitress, let her be a waitress.

Once Natalia's knees were bandaged, the three of us watched *Mickey Mouse Clubhouse,* because that's what happened to be on when Natalia turned on the TV. We thought it was funny that we were tenth-graders, and yet we were being entertained by Donald Duck and Mickey.

"I'm a Boy Scout, you know," Roby said out of the blue.

"Why, yes, Roby, I do know," Natalia said. "I went to that car race thing of yours."

"The Pinewood Derby," Roby said. "That was years ago."

"Why'd you bring up being a Boy Scout?" I asked.

"Natalia falling. Crisis situations." He sat tall. "I know what to do in an emergency, is all."

"Cool," I said.

"I know how to use a compass. If you drop me in the wilderness, I guarantee I'll find my way out."

I almost said something salty, like how I'd keep that in mind the next time I found myself lost in the woods. Instead, I gave him a thumbs-up.

"I'll be an Eagle Scout when I'm a senior," Roby said.

"Maybe you two don't realize it, but it's a pretty big deal."

Natalia put her hand on his knee. "It is. It totally is. You're amazing, Roby."

A flush rose on Roby's face. "Thank you. That's really nice of you to say."

My eyes went to Natalia's hand, still on Roby's knee. I should have been a Boy Scout. Why wasn't I a Boy Scout?

I grabbed the bag of Tostitos. "Chips, anyone?"

Natalia moved her hand off Roby's knee and plunged it into the bag.

Good girl, I thought. Then I tried to rewind my brain and take the "good girl" back, because I remembered, suddenly, a Reddit article I'd stumbled on once while searching for sexy pictures.

"If you want a girl to be naughty in bed and do ANYTHING YOU WANT, just whisper 'good girl' into her ear," the article claimed. "The more you praise her, the naughtier she'll be."

Mickey Mouse Clubhouse ended and *DuckTales* came on. Roby stood and said, "We should let you rest."

"I am resting," Natalia said.

"Plus we should go back for my bike and the skateboards," said Roby. "Come on, Paul."

"Is it *DuckTales*?" Natalia said. She gazed at me. "You hate *DuckTales*, and that's why you're leaving?"

"Are you kidding?" I said. "I love *DuckTales*."

"But my stuff," Roby said. "And Paul, your bike's at my house."

"Roby. Chill. If you want to go, go."

Roby glanced from me to Natalia, then sat down heavily. "Fine," he said. "I'll stay."

chapter thirteen

Roby and Natalia and I became a threesome, but not in a pervy way. Roby had a crush on Natalia. It was obvious. I had a crush on her, too, and if I thought for half a second that I had a chance with her, I'd have owned up to it.

But Natalia had a crush on a guy named Cyrus, as it turned out. So.

Natalia hung out with us cuz we were funny boys and kind boys and kicked-back boys, and we hung out with her for the same reasons in reverse. And yet, *in addition* to those admirable qualities, Natalia was also 100 percent totally and fully gorgeous. Shiny brown hair that hung all the way to her waist. Brown skin. Soft skin. Soft skin that I bet was super soft in certain soft places. Brown hair, brown skin, and the biggest brown eyes you've ever seen, framed with dark feathery lashes.

God made her right, shimmy, shimmy, Cocoa Puffs.

Wait, not Cocoa Puffs because she's brown. Also not because she's *not* brown. Fuck that shit. Natalia is shimmy shimmy Cocoa Puffs because she *is*, and because it's fun to say.

Sometimes Natalia curled her hair. When she did, it bounced in spirals that grazed the middle of her back. Sometimes she wore it in braids, and when I tugged one and said, "Bye, Felicia," she swatted me. Sometimes she wore it in a ponytail. Sometimes in a high poof, and she'd tilt her head from side to side to make the poof flop like a dinging bell.

"I could stash an egg in there," Roby said.

"A peach," I countered.

"A cantaloupe," Roby said. He pulled his fist to his side. "Ka-ching!"

"What are you ka-chinging?" I said, laughing.

Roby man-danced. "Cantaloupe beats peach. Cantaloupe beats peach!"

Sometimes Natalia wore sweats and big T-shirts with

Tupac on them or the dude from *Good Burger*. Sometimes leggings – I liked her "leggings days" a lot – and sometimes skirts. I liked her "skirt days" a *lot* a lot.

When winter came, Natalia wore jeans and fuzzy sweaters and a bright red pom-pom hat. When the snow melted and green shoots started peeking up from the ground, Natalia wore shorts that showed off her butt and cropped tops that showed off her stomach, which was both flat and the slightest bit pudgy at the same time. Not a six-pack. Not even a four-pack. She'd pat her belly after we chowed down on Chick-fil-A and call it her "food baby," and because she had a thing for Chick-fil-A's chicken nuggets, Roby and I sometimes called her "Chicken Nugget."

Natalia's toenails were always painted to match her fingernails, which were acrylics, a term I learned from her. Basically, they were fake nails. Mom thought it was nuts, Natalia's passion for long fake fingernails.

"How can she do anything with those nails?" she'd say. "How can she type or play the piano or whatever?"

"She doesn't play the piano," I told her.

"Why not?"

"And I don't know how she manages to type, but she does. Chill out, lady."

I didn't tell Mom how frickin' amazing Natalia's fingernails felt when she ran them through my hair. She didn't do it in a flirty way, but more like I was an oversize puppy and she was plucking fleas from my fur.

Roby's parents gave him a car for his sixteenth birthday, a used black Volvo sedan. According to North Carolina state law, Roby could only have one passenger under the age of twenty-one for the first six months after getting his license, so no joyriding with me and Natalia right off the bat. Also, sophomores weren't granted spots in the high-school parking lot, so for now he wasn't even driving himself to school. Or driving Natalia, thank god, as I would have felt really jealous.

Roby was proud of his car and kept it clean, and on the last Saturday in March, he and Natalia and I hauled buckets of soapy water onto his driveway and scrubbed it from bumper to bumper. Natalia wore a bikini, and soap bubbles glistened on her skin, and I had to work hard to keep my eyes from roving where they shouldn't.

(My mama taught me well. I know where to keep my gaze. Unless the girl looks away, in which case you can peek at her tits if you're quick.)

When I met Natalia in Ms. Summers's class, I'd pegged her as a pretty girl who was smart and shy. She was all of those things for sure, but she was also salty as fuck. In May, I turned sixteen, and Natalia baked a cake and brought it to school and made everyone in the cafeteria sing to me. Then, with everyone still watching, she challenged me to a burping contest – and won.

The day was warm and sunny, so Natalia, Roby, and I spent the last half of lunch outside on the quad. Natalia's best female friend, Kahlia, joined us, as did Gertrude. Also this guy Monty, who was a slacker and a stoner, and his friend Cyrus, the guy Natalia had a crush on. I didn't like Cyrus as a matter of principle, but Monty was all right.

Monty pulled out his kendama, which is a toy consisting of a wooden ball connected to a wooden handle by a sturdy piece of string. The handle is shaped like a cross, with each of the four end points offering a different challenge. You start with the ball below the handle, dangling from the string. You flick your wrist to toss the ball into the air, and then you catch it on top of the handle, or you try to.

Monty was good, manipulating the handle to pull off increasingly complicated sequences.

"It's all in the knees," he said. He gathered the ball, handle, and string and passed the kendama to me. "Go for it, birthday boy."

I tossed the ball and missed. I tossed it and missed again.

"Start with your hand lower," Monty coached.

I did, and this time the ball landed on the handle with a satisfying *thonk*.

"Nice!" exclaimed Monty. "Keep at it. Yeah, like that."

As I practiced, Cyrus grilled me about why I didn't yet have my driver's license. I shot Roby a look to say, *Do you believe this kid, riding me on my birthday?*

"Dude, I turned sixteen this morning," I told Cyrus. "Give me time."

"But you don't even have your learner's permit, do you?" Cyrus pressed.

The ball, which I'd just landed, toppled and fell.

"Am I right?" Cyrus said. "You don't even have your learner's?"

"So give me *more* time," I said, earning me laughs from Natalia and Gertrude.

How did Cyrus know I didn't have my learner's? Not that it was any of his business. Not that I had to defend myself or my choices.

But who told him?

I shot Roby another look.

"I'm sixteen and I don't have my license yet," Gertrude said.

"Why not?" Cyrus asked.

"Because it's not that big of a deal to me," she said. "Why do you care?"

"I don't," Cyrus said. "But I'm getting my license the day – the *morning* – I turn sixteen."

"Well, bully for you," Gertrude said, and I could have hugged her for being so weird and awkward and Gertrude-ish. For sticking up for me, even by saying "bully for you."

I landed the wooden ball on the handle. I tossed the ball, twisted my wrist, and landed it again on the opposite end. I said, "Hey, did anyone see that?"

No, of course not. Everyone saw – heard – Cyrus announce my lack of even a learner's permit, but my kendama trick? Everyone missed my kendama trick, which unlike getting a stupid learner's permit or driver's license actually mattered in this life-world-being-a-human thing.

Yeah. No. Even I wasn't buying my bullshit.

I tossed the ball and didn't catch it.

"Rough," said Monty, who was paying attention now that I was back to sucking. Monty got his driver's license last semester, earlier than anyone else that I knew of. I'd seen him driving around with a carful of guys, so that meant he'd moved on from a provisional license to the real deal. Either that or he didn't mind breaking the law.

I felt the weight of Natalia's gaze. Was I blushing? Was I, god forbid, looking fragile and/or blinking too much? I despised myself for being so weird and anxious and Paul-ish, but guess what? The prospect of getting my license *did* stress me out. Why?

Because being behind the wheel of a four-thousand-pound hunk of metal sounded like a bad idea.

Because being behind the wheel of a four-thousand-pound hunk of metal with my mother sitting next to me, judging and gasping and overreacting, sounded like a terrible idea.

Because being behind the wheel of *my mother's* four-thousand-pound hunk of metal, with my mother sitting next to me – gasping and overreacting – sounded flat-out unbearable. Because my mom's car is a stick shift, not an automatic, and that means stalling out and panicking and stalling out again, and people honking and getting pissed, and the car possibly *rolling backward down a hill* if, due to fate and bad luck, I had to stop at a red light at the *top* of a hill.

Just no, okay?

It's too much.

"Anyway, I have my bike," I muttered. I flicked the ball, missed, and tried again.

And then Natalia was at my side. She'd come up beside me, and I wanted to impress her, especially with fucking Cyrus standing around being such a fucking jerk.

"I nailed 'around the world'!" I said. "Around the world" with a kendama meant catching the ball on each of the four stations of the handle consecutively, without the ball falling in between.

"You did?" Monty said.

"Seventeen times, man, all in a row! That's why they call me Big Paul."

Natalia laughed, music to my ears. "What? Who calls you Big Paul?"

"Everyone."

"No," she said. "No one calls you Big Paul, Paul. Sorry."

"They could."

"They don't."

"*You* could."

"Not gonna."

I passed the kendama to Natalia. "You try."

She caught the ball on her first attempt.

"Sweet!" I said.

"You're a natural!" said Monty.

She tossed the ball and missed, four times in a row.

"Ah, well. You win some, you lose some," I said.

"Says the birthday-boy-turned-philosopher," drawled Cyrus. "You come up with that pearl of wisdom on your own?"

"Fuck off," I told him. To Natalia, I said, "If at first you don't succeed, or if at first you *do* succeed, but later you crash and burn —"

"Har-har," Natalia said. She tried again and missed. Again.

I gave her a noogie. "That's okay, Big Natalia. I mean Little Natalia. I mean Natalia. We love you anyway."

She stuck out her tongue. I grinned. I grinned, and I realized I felt better, because ... I don't know. Maybe I did love Natalia, and screw Cyrus, for real. The kids around me on the quad, I'd been in high school with them for two years now. For the most part I liked them. For the most part, I liked me. And if at first you don't succeed? Try, try again.

Gertrude strode over and stuck out her hand. "Give me that," she demanded.

Natalia passed her the kendama.

She caught it her very first time. She caught it her second time and her third time, too. She nodded, pleased, and handed it over to Monty.

"Did you see that?" she asked me and Natalia.

"Dude," said Natalia.

"You rocked it," I said.

She gave a satisfied nod. "And that is why they call me Big Gertrude."

chapter
fourteen

The school year ended.

"We're juniors now," I told Roby after the bell rang at the end of our last class. "Juniors! Can you believe it?"

"Amazing," he said.

"I know!" I said.

We celebrated by running nekkid around Roby's neighborhood. Yep, you heard that right. We were the Naked Road Warriors of Junior Awesomeness.

Natalia and Kahlia started it. I was spending the night at Roby's. Kahlia was spending the night at Natalia's. I guess they ran naked across Dupont Golf

Course, and I say "I guess" because I wasn't there to see it, though believe me, I would have loved to have been.

They texted us about it, everyone looped in on the same text chain:

So much fun! Kahlia dared me to.
NO YOU SLUT
Natalia bleeping dared *me*!
Epic end to an epic year! Woot!

"Do you think they're drunk?" Roby asked, lowering his phone.

"Does Natalia *get* drunk?" I asked. She'd never gotten drunk around me. *I'd* never gotten drunk around me.

He shrugged. "Maybe that's what she and Kahlia do?"

Another text came in from Natalia:

Where my boys at? We wantz to seeeeee you!

"Drunk," Roby said.

I tugged the hairs at the back of my neck. "Maybe we should get drunk, too?"

"On what?" said Roby. "I'm not saying I'm against the idea, because I'm not. Just ... ?"

We went down to his parents' wine cellar. Or more like wine closet, a small windowless room in the basement.

"Not exceedingly drunk," I suggested. "Just slightly drunk."

Our phones pinged:

But you have to take the dare too
BOTH of you
(yes Paul I'm talking to U, u wimp)

"Hey, now," I protested. My cheeks grew warm.

"She calls 'em as she sees 'em," said Roby. "I admire that in a girl."

Run around nekkid. I don't care where.
Take pics for evidence.
Then come hang with me and Kahlia.

On our screens came dots, then no dots, then dots. Then:

We'll show you ours if you show us yours . . .
wink wink nudge nudge

"Whoa," I said.

Roby tugged at the crotch of his pants. "Did *they* take pics? Is that what Natalia is saying?"

Natalia sent one last text. It said:

Signing off. Stay in touch!

Then a string of *x*'s, which I think are supposed to be kisses.

Roby slid his phone into his pocket and picked up a bottle of wine. "This doesn't look crazy expensive, does it?"

"Dude, I have no clue."

"I don't think my parents would mind," said Roby. "It's just wine. We're not driving anywhere."

"Hell no. I don't even have my license yet," I said. "Not even my learner's." I looked at Roby pointedly. I still hadn't asked him if he was the one who'd shared that info with Cyrus.

"That's right," Roby said. "We're safe boys."

"And yet we're also brave boys."

Roby opened the bottle of wine, which had a screw cap, so he was right that it couldn't have been crazy expensive. "Risky boys."

"Soon to be naked-as-a-jaybird boys?" I said. "Are we really going to do this?"

"We can't let Natalia and Kahlia one-up us, can we?" Roby asked.

"Absolutely not," I said.

Plus, pictures, I'm sure both of us were thinking. *Of nakedness. Girl nakedness. Frickin' Natalia and Kahlia nakedness.*

Roby and I chugged the wine, passing the bottle back and forth and becoming increasingly wired or tipsy or both.

"It tastes like grape juice," I said.

"It is grape juice."

"How did it turn into wine?"

"Because of Jesus, dumbshit." Roby grinned at his wit. "More questions?"

"Yeah. Did you talk to Cyrus about me?"

"What?"

The question popped out on its own. I hadn't planned it. But now that it was out there...

"How'd Cyrus know that I don't have my learner's yet?" I said. "That day on the quad. Did you tell him?"

"Paul. No."

"If you did, just tell me."

"I can't believe you think that," Roby said. He paced back and forth in the wine closet, swigging from the wine bottle. "That's your business, man. Only a jerk would go around sharing your personal business with an asswipe like Cyrus."

"*Is* Cyrus an asswipe?" I asked. "I'd like to think so, but I'm lacking any real evidence."

"He said Gertrude has a penis."

"What?"

"And that she needs to get laid."

"Have you told Natalia this? You should tell Natalia."

"I did," he said.

"What'd she say?"

"No, I mean I told Cyrus that you don't have your learner's license. It was me." He thrust the wine bottle at me. "Paul, man, I'm really sorry."

I swigged what was left and banged the bottle down. Not loud enough to wake his parents, but nevertheless with oomph.

"It was a dick move," he admitted.

"Uh, yeah," I said.

"I don't even know why I did it."

"I do. To make me look bad in front of Natalia."

He frowned. "But Natalia already knew."

He was right. Natalia did already know.

But I was right, too. By sharing my deficiencies with Cyrus, Roby's goal had been to make me look like less of a man in front of Natalia. I knew this because on some level I understood Roby's impulse. If the situation had been reversed, I might have done the same.

"You know what?" I said. I yanked my shirt over my head. "It's time."

"Shit," Roby said. "Is it?"

"It is."

We stripped to our boxers. We looked everywhere but at each other, but even so I saw that my quads were twice as big as Roby's.

"We'll go to the stop sign and back," Roby declared. "Half a block."

"But not in the direction of Natalia's house," I clarified.

"God, no."

We tiptoed upstairs. Every hair on my body stood at attention. I felt loose and a little sloppy, but also hyperaware of every sound and sensation.

Roby opened the front door. He whispered, "You ready?"

I gestured at his cell phone, which he clutched with tight fingers. "Why are you bringing your phone?"

"We have to take a picture, don't we? For proof!"

He slipped off his boxers in one jerky movement, and he was off, his pale bottom flashing in the moonlight.

"Fuck," I muttered. I tugged off my boxers and raced after him. The cool night air swooshed around me, everywhere, everywhere. I sped up, whooping as I approached the stop sign.

"You idiot!" Roby called, laughing. "Shut up!"

I passed Roby, slapped the stop sign, and changed directions, bolting back to the house. Up the driveway, through the door, a fast swipe for my boxers. Then downstairs to the basement and into my clothes. I grinned and flung myself on the sofa.

"Naked we came into the world, and naked we will leave," Roby said when he joined me. He hopped on one foot as he struggled into his joggers.

"Nothing wrong with naked," I said.

"Nothing wrong with naked," he echoed. "That was awesome. Wasn't that awesome?"

"Fuck yeah."

"Would we have done that last summer? No way."

"Last summer, we were lowly sophomores. Now we rule the world."

"Shout-out to juniors! Yah!"

I spotted his phone on the coffee table. "Oh, shit."

"What 'oh, shit'?" Roby said. "Why are you hitting me with 'oh, shit'?"

"We forgot to take pictures. We didn't take any dick pics!"

Roby looked stricken. Then his face contorted, and he cracked up.

"Ah, man!" he said. "How are we going to see Natalia and Kahlia's pictures if we don't show them any of ours?"

"How can we show them any of ours if we don't have any at all?"

"How can we have any pudding if we don't eat our meat?"

We rolled around, laughing. We were ridiculous.

chapter fifteen

Many hours later, or maybe just one, I awoke to Roby shaking my shoulder. "Kahlia texted," he said. "They're at the playground."

We snuck out and walked down the dark road to Roby and Natalia's old elementary school. Natalia and Kahlia were there, as well as Gertrude and a girl named Helen. Helen was into K-pop and sometimes wore footie pajamas to school, but managed to never get dress-coded.

She wasn't wearing footie pajamas now. She was wearing normal clothes, like the rest of us. We sat on top of the monkey bars, a warm breeze wafting over us. Fireflies twinkled everywhere. It felt, already, like summer.

With no streetlamps polluting the night sky, the stars glittered like crazy and the moon was a crisp white crescent. The six of us talked about music and movies and Natalia's summer nannying job in Atlanta. She was leaving the next weekend and would be gone till the middle of August.

"I'm doing it as a favor to my mom's college roommate," Natalia explained. "She has nine-year-old twins, and she just had a baby."

"You're being shipped out as free labor?" Roby said.

"I'm getting paid," Natalia said with a laugh.

"It's a terrible idea," I said. "Don't go."

"In July, the family's taking me to Martha's Vineyard, then to New York," she said. "I'm stoked."

"Even with twins to take care of? And a baby?" Roby said.

"Lena's nine," Natalia said. "It's not as if I don't know what I'm getting into."

"Exactly," Roby said.

"Where in New York?" Helen asked. "Manhattan?"

"Yeah," Natalia said. "Street performers! Hot dogs!"

"You've been to New York before?" I asked.

She flicked my head. "I've been lots of places, silly Paul."

"I love New York," Helen said. She swung her feet back and forth below the monkey bars. "I want to live there one day."

"For me, it's Paris," Natalia said. "Or anywhere in France."

"*France?*" I said.

She gave me a funny look.

"You'd move to France?" I said. "For real?"

"Why do you think I'm taking five years of French?" she said.

I wouldn't mind visiting France, but I couldn't imagine moving there. To be fair, I couldn't imagine moving anywhere.

"Wouldn't Lena miss you?" I asked.

"She could come visit."

"I'd come visit," Roby volunteered. To Helen, he said, "New York, too."

"I am totally in for New York," I said. "Up my sauce game, yo. Swag this boy out."

Helen turned to Natalia. "What is he talking about?"

Natalia rolled her eyes. "Clothes, shoes, you name it."

"I'll name it," I said. I ticked off brands on my fingers.

"Gucci, Chanel, Ferragamo. Prada. Armani. Ooo, ooo! Off-White! Flagship boutique, yaz!"

"Paul, I like clothes too," Natalia said.

"I prefer the term 'apparel.' And don't forget jewelry. Ice, ice, baby."

"But clothes don't make the man. You know that, right? That you don't have to prove yourself with 'sauce'?"

She made air quotes. I wasn't sure whether to feel offended, embarrassed, or pleased.

"Well, that's lucky, given that my sauce level isn't as high as I'd like," I said.

"That so?" Roby said. He jerked his chin at my hat. "What brand's your bucket hat?"

"*Comme des Garçons.* Bite me."

Later, Gertrude brought out a blunt and offered it around.

"Sure, why not?" I said.

I was nervous, but I'd heard that weed was good for anxiety. That getting to a place of feeling mellow was kind of the point.

I held the blunt with my thumb and forefinger and inhaled, the way I'd seen Gertrude do. The smell of weed turned into the flavor of weed, sweet and thick. I held the smoke in my lungs for a good ten seconds, then blew it out. No coughing, no sputtering. It was my first time to smoke anything, weed or nicotine, and I was proud of how I handled myself.

The joint circulated among us. I watched the end glow red as Roby took a drag. He coughed and cracked up, and coughed some more. I thumped his back and said, "You okay?" He nearly toppled off the monkey bars, but Gertrude and I pulled him upright.

He took another hit. *"Paul,"* he said. *"Pa-aul."* There was something slightly off about his face. *"Paul-l-l-l,* your name is facking weird. Why am I just now noticing?"

"You're stoned," Gertrude said.

"Am I? Whoa," said Roby.

The first time the joint went around, Natalia took a small hit, after which she coughed into her fist. When it came to her again, she shook her head. Helen also passed, so Kahlia shrugged and lifted it to her lips. She, Gertrude, Roby, and I passed it back and forth, its ember brightening and dimming.

I soaked in the fullness of Natalia's lips, the gleam of her dark hair spilling over her shoulders. *Remember this,* I told myself, searing her image into my brain. I couldn't return to this moment. In fact, it had already passed. But I could store the memory forever.

Roby and Gertrude discussed Cyrus's assholery. Helen jumped in and told a story about last fall's homecoming dance.

"Cyrus saw me and Monty dancing and called Monty a chubby-chaser," she said.

"What a jerk!" Natalia said.

"He really is," Gertrude said. She took Helen's hand. "And you're perfect, Helen. Fuck him."

"Or don't," Natalia said. She shuddered. "I low-key can't believe I ever had feelings for him."

She caught me staring at her. She said, "What?"

"Nothing, just enjoying the view," I said.

We gazed at each other. She smiled at me just with her lips. Her teeth were still there, obviously, but they were hidden. Secret.

It felt like a momentous observation, and if I'd put it into words, it would have been to remark on how we all have hidden smiles. We all have secret selves. And somehow I'd have tied "teeth" into it. Bright white crescents, like pieces of the moon. No, bright white Chiclets, because Chiclets were pieces of gum, and a person's gums were what held their teeth in place. Teeth as white as crisp linen, as moist and secret as someone lying naked beneath crisp linens.

chapter
sixteen

That summer, weed became an important part of my lifestyle. Gertrude led me down the garden path, and I had no interest in turning back. Any time anyone offered me a j, I was in.

Gertrude taught me to cover the scent with peanut butter, which worked beautifully except for the time Mom caught me eating it straight from the jar. But I rallied, waving my goopy spoon and saying, "Protein, Ma. Get with the program."

"Just don't double-dip," Mom replied, wrinkling her nose. I often get that particular wrinkled-nose look from her: mild revulsion mixed with fondness, as if she can't quite believe she made me, this large, sometimes stinky, always untidy boy who *does* double-dip and who chugs orange juice out of the carton even though she begs me not to.

Gertrude introduced me to smoking. Soon after, Monty introduced me to dabbing. Given the choice, I'd rather dab, since dabbing means I don't have to use the peanut trick or change my shirt the second I get home.

Roby, on the other hand, didn't like dabbing. We disagreed about other drug habits, too. Over the summer I realized that drugs weren't nearly as scary as I'd built them up to be, and my general stance was that I'd try anything once, or almost anything.

Not Roby. Roby worried about ruining his brain cells and doing permanent harm to his body, shit like that.

For example, one weekend he and I decided to get high on over-the-counter Robitussin. It made us both sick, and we threw up all over the place. It was gnarly. But before we got sick, everything felt mellow and floaty.

Me? I liked it. I felt like I was wrapped in cotton gauze, like nothing could reach through and hurt me.

Roby, on the other hand, said, "Never again. I'll stick to weed, thanks." He claimed we'd poisoned ourselves and that throwing up was our bodies' way of getting the poison out. He was all, "Was it worth it just to be high for five minutes?" To which I was all, "Were we, though? Were we even high at all?"

(For the record, yes. I admit that it *is* possible to get faded on dextromethorphan, which is the "DXM" part of Robitussin DXM. Which is what Roby and I took. But when I later found out you're supposed to drink cough syrup with codeine, the kind you need a prescription for, I felt like an idiot.)

One weekend Roby and I went to a party at Torin's house, and I sipped lean for the first time. I figured out why it's called lean. It's because when you get high on it, you feel off-balance, like you're leaning. Also, you see stuff that possibly isn't really there.

I told Roby how funny and awesome it was, because I wanted him to try it for himself. He said, "Paul, watching you hallucinate is boring as fuck. If you want to chill, great. If you're going to drink your stupid purple drank, I'm going to take off." And he did. I kept drinking my stupid purple drank, and he left. The plan had been for me to sleep at Roby's house, but I crashed at Torin's instead.

Roby discouraged me from xans as well. He gave me a speech about how addictive they were and made me promise not to make a habit out of taking them. Same with cocaine.

"Cocaine is sometimes cut with meth, you idiot," he told me. "If you do coke, you're probably going to do meth and become even more of a tweaker. You're anxious as fuck already, Paul. You do not need to do a stimulant. Understand?"

But see, that's why I love that kid. I can get a proper roasting from him and still be good friends. When others roast me, it hurts.

Take Monty. I liked Monty, but when Monty came down on me, it seemed like his goal was to hurt my feelings, not to gently make me aware of something it was in my best interest to know, like that my hair looked bad or my bracelet was too big.

Roby was honest in a kind way. If I was being stupid, he told me. But he also talked me up, telling me my fashion sense was dope and that I had good taste in music. I did the same thing for him. Win-win.

Bottom line, we're real with each other. In fifty years, we'll be like those old men who spend hours at all-day-breakfast diners. We'll have big ears and tufting sprouts of nose hair, and we'll guffaw at everything the other says. *Heh-heh-heh, you know it, Roby. Pass the damn ham.*

chapter
seventeen

It was the middle of August before I knew it, hot, humid, and buggy. On the plus side, Natalia had returned from her summer of nannying. I hadn't seen her yet, but she'd texted to let me know. On the minus side, summer was ending and soon the school year would grind back into gear. Back on the plus side, once we were in school, I'd see Natalia every day of the week. I'd missed that girl.

Maybe Roby sensed that I'd been thinking about her. Maybe he'd been thinking about her, too. Or maybe he wanted to get in one last day of hanging out together, just the two of us, before school started and we fell into our school routines. Whatever the reason, he called me right as I was heading out to bike to his house and suggested we meet at Spring Creek Park instead.

At first, I didn't get it. I'd assumed that I'd go over to Roby's, and that we'd go over to Natalia's together. Welcome her back, hear about New York, allow Lena to bring us ice-cold Cokes and assorted snacks.

On further reflection, however, maybe I didn't want my first time seeing Natalia to be a reunion of the Roby-Paul-Natalia threesome. Maybe it was time to strike out on my own, and if not today, then soon.

I arrived at the park to find Roby waiting for me at the bike rack.

"Wassup?" I said, giving him some dap. For us, that meant a handshake, a quick squeeze, a finger slide, and a snap, topped off with a fist bump. It's an art form.

Roby's knuckles met mine. "Hey, man."

At first we stuck to the park's perimeter, shuffling around in our low-hanging joggers and loose-fitting extra-large T-shirts. My shirt was only slightly loose, as my shoulders had grown broader over the summer and I'd been doing push-ups every morning to bulk up.

Roby continued to wear an extra-large as an act of

self-determination. He hasn't given up hope on a late-in-life growth spurt.

Eventually we stopped trying to look cool and headed over to the playground equipment. Once there, we did what you're supposed to do at a playground. We played.

First we tackled an oversize disk suspended a couple of feet above the ground. It was like a hamster wheel for humans. When we walked on it, it moved beneath us. The faster we walked, the faster it turned, and Roby and I laughed our asses off every time we were flung from the wheel onto the rubber mulch below.

After wearing ourselves out on the human hamster wheel, we climbed to the top of a giant statue of a dinosaur. It was twenty feet tall. Maybe thirty.

I was sweating by the time I made it to the dinosaur's head, and I'm a strapping sixteen-year-old. The other kids playing on the dinosaur were younger and smaller, the elementary-school crowd. The dinosaur's tail had ridges in it, like a ladder. That part was easy to climb. After the tail came the dinosaur's rear legs, which were trickier. The carved muscles bulged out, and there weren't many nubs to grab or outcroppings to wedge your feet against.

This one kid, though. He was maybe six. He wore a short-sleeved button-down shirt tucked into khaki dress shorts. A brown belt circled his Froot Loop of a waist. His shoes were church shoes.

I knew so much about this kid just from looking at him. Like that his mom still chose his outfits and refused to let him pick out his own clothes. That she was super strict and probably said things like "Don't even think about untucking your shirt, young Sebastian!" And that his name might actually have been Sebastian or, worse, Gaylord.

Dang, I hope his name wasn't Gaylord.

I also knew, with a tightening sensation in my heart, that he was the kid other kids cut in front of, like when he was in line to go down the slide or get a drink from the water fountain. Maybe he said, "Hey, no cutting!" but no one cared, not even the teachers, because he was *that kid.* The kid who made other kids thankful for whatever shred of power they possessed, no matter how small. The kid who made other kids feel scared in the twistiest parts of their stomachs if they asked themselves why they shunned him. Although they never did ask themselves that, I'm sure.

I felt bad for him. Irrationally, I even felt responsible

for him. What if by a roll of the dice he'd been my brother? What if Willow, my baby sister who died before she was born, had been a boy instead of a girl? What if she hadn't died, but instead turned out to be as cringey as this guy?

The kid, who I'm going to call Sebastian, not Gaylord, broke free of the ring of kids surrounding the dinosaur. He strode closer and planted his hands on his hips. His shorts billowed around his legs like sails.

"Uh-oh," Roby said under his breath.

But I give mad props to Gaylord. I mean Sebastian. He scaled the tail of the dinosaur, no problem. Then he huffed and grunted and hauled himself over the dinosaur's leg, his white thighs clenching the stone and the tip of his pink tongue poking out of his mouth.

"You got this, bruh," I called down to him.

"Yeah, man," said Roby. "Grab that notch on your left. Your other left. Sweet!"

On the ground, kids made visors out of their hands and squinted up at us, monitoring Sebastian's progress.

"You're gon-na fall!" one boy jeered.

A girl pulled a cherry lollipop out of her mouth and cried, "I see his underwear! His Thomas the Tank Engine underwear!"

I clenched my jaw. I wore Thomas the Tank Engine underwear once upon a time. Tighty-whities with red trim, with Thomas's blue engine on the butt. I imagined standing where the lollipop girl stood. In my mind I saw what she saw: Sebastian's huge shorts poofing around his legs, and Thomas the Tank Engine's round moon face shining forth, his glazed smile stretched across his butt.

"We can see your undies!" three kids chorused. "We can see your undies!"

I whacked the dinosaur's head. "Scram!" I yelled.

"Scram?" Roby repeated.

To Sebastian, who was less than a yard away, I said, "You're so close."

Roby extended his hand, but Sebastian ignored it.

Shit. I'm making it out like it was this big drama. It was, but it wasn't.

His loafer slipped when he was a foot and a half from the top. He scrambled for purchase, but the smooth stone gave him nothing, and he slid-bounced-bumped all the way to the soft mulch below. He landed in a sprawl of marshmallow limbs and humiliation, and everybody laughed.

Now came the real test, even if Sebastian didn't know it.

"Don't do it," I urged, balancing on one knee and gripping the dinosaur's teeth. "Do not let them see you cry."

"Too late," Roby said flatly.

Tears streamed down the kid's face. Snot bubbled from his nose. His mother ran over and hauled him up, barking, "What were you thinking? You know you're not big enough to climb the dinosaur. You *know* that!"

Later I spotted Sebastian on the swing set. Only, he wasn't swinging. He sat on the black rubber seat with his head bowed and his fingers clutching the chains. Every so often, he kicked at the dirt.

Next to the regular swings was a row of bucket swings. I loped over, grabbed a set of chains, and hoisted myself up so that my sneakers rested on top of the bucket.

"Don't even, you idiot," said Roby.

"I'm no idiot," I said. "I'm reliving the glory days."

"Which glory days?"

I wormed my left foot through the left leg hole. I bore my weight with my arms and fished for the second hole. Sebastian watched from under a swoop of hair.

"Wooo, doggy!" I cried. My grip slipped, and I slid deeper into the bucket. My joggers bunched up. The rubber leg holes cut into my skin. I thrashed and tried to unwedge myself. "Roby? A little help?"

Roby fished his phone out of his pocket. "I've got to show this to Natalia. She's back in town, you know."

"Roby, don't." I tried to hump my way out of the bucket seat as Roby circled around behind me. "For real, don't be a dick."

There was a click, along with more laughter.

"Do not send that to Natalia," I said, on the edge of panic. "Please."

"Why not? Do you like her, is that it?"

"Fuck off. Of course I like her."

"Yeah, but do you *like* her like her?"

"Are you in seventh grade?"

"Answer the question."

So this is how it's going to go down, I thought. *We're finally going to have this conversation, which, yes, we need to have, while I'm ass-down in a bucket swing.*

"I know you have a crush on her," Roby said. "Admit it."

"*You* have a crush on her. *You* admit it." I flailed and kicked.

"I told you last year how much I liked Natalia. What I don't get is why you're not respecting that."

Roby should get "dibs" on Natalia because he

claimed her first, that's what he was arguing. I'm not convinced it works that way. Natalia has dibs on herself, that's what I think.

Roby hovered his thumb over his phone. "Sending," he warned.

"Wait!" I twisted and jerked my hips until I was facing Sebastian. "Little dude, come here. I swear I'm not a creeper."

Sebastian glanced at his mom, who was talking to some other ladies. He hopped off his swing and cautiously approached.

I shifted, trying to get my boxers out of my ass crack. "You've never had to choose between your best friend and a girl," I said to him. "Amirite?"

"So you *do* like her," Roby said.

"If I had to choose, I'd choose my friend," said the kid.

"No, wrong," I said. "People aren't carnival prizes. You don't have to choose."

"You could, though," Roby said. "You could choose me."

"I do. I choose you both." My legs had lost all circulation. I could no longer feel my toes. "But Roby, I can't walk away and not even try for Natalia. You get that, right?"

"Where does that leave you and me?" he said. "May the best man win?"

"It's not about winning."

"You sure?" He pushed a button on his phone, and I heard the *whoosh* of pixels flying through the air.

"Hey!"

"Natalia wants to know what you're doing in a bucket swing," Roby said.

I thrust my torso back and forth.

"She wants to know if you're stuck, and if I'm going to smack your bingo."

I made a guttural sound. Sebastian looked alarmed. I beckoned him closer and said, "Grab hold of the seat."

He did.

I said, "Good. Now try to keep it steady."

Sebastian wrapped both arms around the bucket part and held on tight. He stuck his tongue out of the side of his mouth the same way he did when he was trying to scale the dinosaur.

Roby tapped at his phone. Soon he would be dead. Soon I'd no longer have to worry about Natalia seeing pictures of my bingo. Just, I had to get out of the damn swing.

I got one foot free. The swing swayed, and Sebastian

swayed with it. Cackling, Roby circled me with his phone.

"Stop taking pictures!"

"I did."

"Finally! Thank you!"

"I switched to video."

"The fuck?!" I glanced at the kid. "Sorry." I worked to free my other knee, and the top edge of the swing dug into my ass crack. "Ow. Shit. Fuck."

"Solid gold," murmured Roby.

With a yank, I freed myself. I went flying and landed ass-down on the dirt. My hat fell off and landed beside me.

"Yay!" said Sebastian.

I tackled Roby and wrested away his phone.

"Too late! Already sent!" he crowed. His smile transformed him into a younger, sweeter version of himself.

I snapped a picture of him doing his victory dance, which involved thrusting his fists toward the ground and lifting his knees like a show pony. Click. Send. *Whoosh!*

"What?" he said, coming to a hard stop. "No!"

I tossed him his phone. "Eat your heart out, Natalia."

junior year

chapter
eighteen

Pretty soon I realized I wasn't going to be able to hide my feelings for Natalia. Not when I was seeing her every day at school. Not with her looking so good and smelling so amazing and smiling at me the way she did.

We had the same lunch period, and it was just us and not Roby, because Roby had second-hour lunch with Monty and Kahlia. Natalia ate with me every day, and she shared her grapes and made me open her milk carton and smell it for her, because the prospect of milk that had gone even the slightest bit sour terrified her. She talked about how much she liked our new media center specialist, who had pink hair and cussed like a sailor, and she told me she might want to be a media center specialist one day. Maybe in North Carolina, maybe in France, who knew?

They weren't related, the grapes and the milk and her dream of being a media center specialist. Just, she was easy to talk to. She suggested books I should read. I introduced her to rappers I hoped she'd like. We shared my headphones and listened to songs together, and when we sat close like that, I sometimes forgot how to breathe.

I wanted desperately to be with her, as a couple. As the weeks passed, I couldn't shake the crazy, tingling thought that she wanted that, too. Like, she held my gaze for longer than she technically needed to. When we ate outside, she kicked off her shoes and propped her feet on my leg. One day she giggled and told me I had a potato chip crumb on my lip, which she then brushed off for me with the pad of her thumb.

It was time, I decided, to be a Man of Action.

So on a clear Saturday morning at the end of September, I biked to her neighborhood, pausing at the end of her street to catch my breath and spray on some cologne, which I brought with me in my backpack. Once

I smelled good and was no longer sweaty, I biked the rest of the way to Natalia's house. My heart was trying to drum its way out of my chest, so I ordered my heart to cool it.

You've got this, I told myself. *Man up.*

I rang the doorbell. Lena opened the door.

"Paul, hi!" she said, her face lighting up. "Want a fruit pop? I made fruit pops."

"Maybe later," I said. "Is Natalia here?"

"No," said Lena.

I stepped partially into the house and glanced up at the staircase. "Are you sure?"

Lena sighed. She craned her neck and called, "Natalia! Paul's here!"

Natalia bounded down the stairs.

"Hey," I said. "You, uh, want to walk around? Maybe hang out at the park?" I needed to get her by herself and away from Lena before I could think about the rest.

"Sure," she said. "Lena, tell Mom I'm going on a walk with Paul. Be back soon!"

I steered her away from Roby's house. She didn't ask why. For a few minutes we talked about our classes, our friends, who'd done what crazy-slash-stupid thing on Snapchat and whose parents actually had a clue about monitoring that shit. (The answer? Nobody's. Teenagers and parents live in different universes.)

The elementary school was deserted. Behind the building was a small courtyard that opened onto a garden decorated with student-made ceramic tiles and lopsided sculptures. In the center of the garden was a wrought-iron bench. I took a seat. Natalia sat down beside me.

I cleared my throat. Natalia pressed her knees together and curled her hands on top of them. She gave me a sweet smile.

I almost fell into the trap of thinking too much about the moment instead of living the moment, which would have been disastrous, because once I start thinking like that, it's hard to stop.

"Um, Paul?" Natalia said.

"I'm going to kiss you now," I blurted. I leaned in and pressed my lips to hers.

She put her hand on my chest and pushed me away. "Whoa, Paul."

Oh, shit. Oh, fuck. Had I gotten everything wrong? Done everything wrong? Turned everything from right into wrong?

"Natalia, I'm so sorry," I said. My heart was back

to trying to leap from my chest. I couldn't breathe normally.

"Paul," Natalia said. She pressed her palm to my chest, and her touch steadied me, until I realized, *Oh, damn, she's touching me, steadying me, pressing her palm against me.*

"No 'sorry,'" she said. "Please don't be sorry."

I placed my hand over hers, capturing it against me. "My heart is pounding so fast," I confessed.

"I can feel," she said.

"So ... why 'whoa'?" I asked.

Her eyes were unlike any other girl's eyes. Yes, I know that other girls have big brown eyes. But Natalia's...

How do you describe the light and love in anyone's eyes, really?

"I don't know," Natalia said. "But it wasn't a bad whoa. More, an 'I want to enjoy this' whoa."

"A slow whoa?"

"A slow whoa."

"Oh, thank god," I said. She laughed.

"Paul, you can't have really thought I was turning you down," she said.

"Want to bet?"

She slid her hand from underneath mine and

placed it on my cheek. She put her other hand on my other cheek.

"I'm going to kiss you now," she said, and she did.

chapter
nineteen

From that point forward, I spent every second I could with Natalia. I was addicted to that girl. I felt like a traitor for not inviting Roby to join us. He had to know what was going down.

But there it was. I ignored Roby's snaps and texts, too.

Usually we hung out in Natalia's room, because Natalia's mom loves me and also she trusts me. When I come over, she plies me with Mexican Coca-Cola and coconut macaroons decorated with green, white, and red stripes. Those are the colors of the Mexican flag, which at first I didn't know. But now I do, just like

I now know that Mexican Coke is better than American Coke because it's made with real sugar instead of high fructose corn syrup.

So anyway, Mrs. Gutierrez loads us up with snacks and then waves us out of the kitchen, saying, "Be good, you two! I know you will!"

Today, after playing not one but two rounds of Trouble with Lena, Natalia shooed her out of her room and pulled me to her bed.

"I'm going to kiss you now," she whispered. It was our favorite joke. I loved that we had a favorite joke.

"Not if I kiss you first." I took her face in my hands and kissed her. Soft. Hard. Warm. Wet. I let one hand drift beneath her shirt. Her skin was silk and honey.

Forget the rest of high school. Forget college. I'd found my calling.

Natalia turned toward me. I felt her hand on my stomach, beneath my T-shirt, and I shuddered. We kissed. We touched. Nothing too serious. We were still pretty innocent in terms of how far things went, but anything and everything was good by me.

"Paul?" she said, eventually pushing herself up. She adjusted her clothes.

I shifted around to conceal my erection, though

the deliciousness of wanting more, wanting her, stayed firm.

"Paul, you need to talk to Roby. You've got to. Please?"

That did the trick. I blinked and said, "Why?"

"You know why. He's your best friend. He misses you."

"No, he doesn't," I said, thinking, *I miss him, too.*

Natalia shoved me. "Paul, don't be stupid."

"What if I am stupid?"

"You're not, so grow up."

I raked my fingers through my hair. "Chill, woman. Man's got to work it out for himself."

"But, Paul," she said. "Odds are your relationship with Roby's going to last longer than your relationship with me."

I stared at her. "Damn, Natalia. Why would you say that?"

"I didn't mean it in a bad way. Just —"

"Do you think we're not going to last long?"

"Paul, no. I am not thinking in any way, shape, or form about the end of us."

"The end of us?" I didn't want there to be an end of us. I didn't understand why she was pushing on it or introducing the possibility. I felt a little shattered. It scared me.

I rose from Natalia's bed, walked to the window, and braced my hands on the sill. I couldn't see Roby's house from here, but the grass in Natalia's yard was the same as the grass in Roby's yard. The sky was the same sky.

What was Roby doing right now? Sleeping? Playing video games? Reading?

"You've been friends with Roby forever," Natalia said, appearing by my side and slipping her arm around my waist. "He needs you and you need him. That's all I'm saying."

"You can't use the idea of us not lasting as a reason to make me go talk to him," I said.

"I'm not making you do anything," she said. Then, right away, "But I hear you. I honestly didn't mean it like a threat or anything."

I sighed. "Okay."

She tilted her head. "Okay, you'll talk to Roby?"

"Okay, I'll talk to Roby."

She nestled up beside me, and I was happy again.

chapter

twenty

I didn't talk to Roby.

I didn't *not* talk to Roby. Just, the situation never arose where it made sense for the two of us to really talk, as in *talk* talk. It's not as if Roby took the time to track me down, either.

We were both to blame. Cool it.

Plus, I had other things on my mind. Listen up, because what I'm about to tell you is real. Touching your own dick is awesome, but when a girl touches your dick ... when a girl you like, maybe even love, touches your dick...

Your "like" turns into "love" real quick, for starters.

Be careful with that one, because true love isn't about fooling around. That said, True Love × Fooling Around = Most Amazing Feeling Ever.

The sensation starts in your dick, grows bigger and stronger, and then, if you're lucky, circles back and ends with your dick. Mom would say that dicks are for private time and so is dick talk, but I'm going in anyway. Wanking off is excellent, but when the same thing happens with a girl, when it happens *because* of a girl, then instead of "ah, yes," it's "AAAAAHHHHHHHHH, YESSSSSS, holy-mother-of-all-that's-holy YAZZZZZZZZZ!"

When it comes to sexy time, guys have it easier than girls. (I am not using the term "sexy time" with a straight face, I'll have you know. I just can't think of a less dumb way to say it.)

I don't know any dude who doesn't rub one out three times daily at least, which means that guys know the lay of the land, if you get my drift. I don't really know how often girls get themselves off, but that's not the point. The point is that as a guy, you know how to touch your dick. Right? Good?

You might need to give your girlfriend a few pointers, however. That's fine. Like, for example, girls' hands are small, because their bodies are small. Since their hands are small, their grip is small. Meaning I had to assure Natalia that my dick wasn't going to break if she rubbed it too hard. I told her that I seriously doubted it was possible for her to rub my dick too hard, but that she had my blessing to try.

"Show me," she said one day up in her bedroom.

I opened my mouth, then shut it. I said, "Uh..."

"Take your hand" – she took my hand – "and put it on your dick." She put my hand on my dick and gave a satisfied nod. She was wearing white shorts, and I could see the line of her panties beneath. She wasn't wearing a shirt, because she'd already pulled it over her head in a single fluid movement. Her bra was lacy and filmy. Sometimes she wears sports bras, because they offer more support or whatever. I like her pretty bras better.

"Show me," she said again, sitting crisscross-applesauce and folding her hands in her lap.

So I did. It was weird, but it was also awesome, especially when she looked to me for permission and then slid her hand underneath mine. She watched my dick as I guided her hand up and down. I watched her face.

"Wow," she said. "You really ... your grip ... your

fingers are a lot stronger than mine." Then, when she took over, "Like this? I'm not hurting you, am I?"

"Natalia, oh my god," I said, and other stuff like that until words were gone and all was sensation.

Afterward I asked her to show me what she liked. How she touched herself, how she wanted to be touched. She did, and I paid hella attention. If you have a girlfriend – when you have a girlfriend – make sure you take care of her just like she takes care of you.

Lecture's over, my brothers. Gimme sum.

Natalia celebrated Christmas in Brevard with Lena and her parents and grandparents and various aunts and uncles and cousins. When I talked to her on the phone this morning, I could hear her relatives in the background. They were loud, and there was lots of laughter.

I spent Christmas in Atlanta with Mom, visiting Grandmom and Granddad. We laughed a lot, too. Just, there's only four of us.

"Paul, come help me with the brownies," Grandmom said the night we arrived, pulling me to the kitchen. She opened the freezer compartment of their fancy refrigerator and pulled out two aluminum foil squares. Inside each square were four homemade brownies wrapped in Saran Wrap. Grandmom is serious about her brownies.

"I always like to have some on hand," she explained. "Wrapping them in Saran Wrap and aluminum foil keeps them fresher."

"Yes, ma'am, Grandmom ma'am," I said.

She laughed and looked at me that way she does, the way that says I'm special.

I freed some dried snot from one nostril. Grandmom recoiled.

"Sorry," I said.

She tsked and handed me a tissue that was "only slightly used." Grandmom's tissues are always "only slightly used," which meant she'd blotted her lipstick with them.

"And wash those hands before having a brownie," she added.

"Of course," I replied.

Later, we sat in Grandmom and Granddad's living room and talked. A fire danced in the fireplace, and a twelve-foot-tall Christmas tree glittered in the corner of the room. Everyone sipped champagne out of Bavarian crystal champagne flutes, and I was super aware that I better not break one.

I told Grandmom and Granddad about Natalia, and Mom chimed in and said what an amazing young woman she was.

"What are her plans for after high school?" Granddad asked.

"College," I said. "Somewhere on the East Coast. She's thinking she wants to study library science."

"I like the sound of that," Granddad said.

"Impressive," Grandmom said.

"She happens to be beautiful, too," Mom said. "Paul, show them a picture."

I pulled out my phone and showed them lots of pictures, and they said really nice things, all of which I agreed with. It made me happy, but it made me miss Natalia like crazy.

I missed Roby, too. I won't lie. But I missed Natalia more. I was glad when it was time to head back home.

We left late on Sunday afternoon. By seven o'clock, we'd crossed the North Carolina state line. As we cruised down the highway in the dark, I thought about Natalia. I thought about life. I thought about everything.

But then...

I slipped into loneliness...

because of all those stars on the other side of the car window.

All that universe. So many unknowns.

Did everyone think about death practically every day, or was it just me? Did everyone wonder why we existed, and if life was nothing but a fluke?

One day, I would die. I could stare at the darkness beyond the car all I wanted. I could lose myself in it, thinking happy thoughts or sad thoughts or in-between thoughts, but when my heart stopped beating and my brain shut off ... then what?

I imagined my body as a collection of atoms arranged in the shape of me, Paul Walden. I imagined those atoms splitting apart and rising into the sky, joining the endless expanse of darkness. I rested my forehead against the window, which was cold against my skin. A hole opened up behind my ribs.

Stop, I told myself. *You're only feeling lonely because you miss Natalia, but you'll see her tomorrow. Don't be whipped.*

I imagined what it would be like if it were me in the driver's seat of the car instead of Mom, and Natalia beside me in the passenger's seat. It was a pipe dream.

My seventeenth birthday was five months away, but I wasn't licensed to drive, nor was I doing anything to become licensed to drive.

But that's why dreams are called dreams, right?

If Natalia and I were driving somewhere on our own, we'd stop at a diner for dinner. We'd laugh and flirt and blow rumpled straw wrappers at each other. Afterward, we'd climb back into the car and play the radio low. The night would stretch on – darkness everywhere, same as every night – and yet the two of us would be together, that one truth changing everything.

chapter

twenty-one

There were mounds of dirty snow all over town, plowed into submission after the last big storm. There was a big heap in the parking lot of Ingles, and when I accompanied Mom on a grocery run, I saw little kids huffing and puffing to the top of it.

Seeing them brought back the memory of cold fingers and toes. Cold nose. Cold knees, raw beneath clammy fabric. When I was their age, I'd play forever in the snow, until Mom finally made me come inside and shed layer after layer of clothing until I was down to my damp and clingy underwear.

Then a warm bath. My skin stung like boiled nuts

when I first lowered myself into the tub, but soon it felt like heaven. Dang, I love a good bath. Always have. Excellent for relaxing, excellent for jacking off, excellent for admiring my naked dick.

When we returned from the grocery store, I toasted bagels and spread them with cream cheese.

"Why, thank you," Mom said when I placed a plate in front of her at the table.

"And you worried I'd never learn to cook," I said.

"I'm not sure toasting a bagel counts as —" She broke off. She took a bite of her bagel and smiled. "Delicious."

I slid into my chair and bit into my own bagel. I nodded happily.

"So, Paul, what's up with Roby these days?" Mom asked. "He hasn't come over once this semester. It's been months since I've seen him."

"It hasn't been months. You're exaggerating," I said. She wasn't.

She lifted one shoulder. "Well? How is he?"

"He's good. He's fine."

"Is he growing into himself, do you think?"

"I don't know what that means."

"Is he happy? Is he comfortable in his own skin?"

"I hope so, since he can't change out of it unless he

turns into that creepy guy from *Silence of the Lambs*." It was a lame-ass attempt to steer the conversation in a different direction, but it was all I had. "'It rubs the lotion on its skin, or it gets the hose again.'"

Mom made a face. "You're cracking out on me, boy."

"Whoa, Mama, don't go snaking my lingo."

Mom considered me. "Back to Roby. Is there something going on I should know about?"

I groaned. "Why the fixation on Roby?"

"Because I miss him. Do you?"

"I see him every day at school."

"That wasn't my question. Are you mad at him?"

"What? No."

"Is he mad at you?"

"Mom."

"Does it have to do with Natalia?"

I put down what was left of my bagel.

"Sometimes it's hard when one person has a girlfriend and the other person doesn't," Mom said.

"I don't want to have this conversation."

"But Roby's your best friend. Best friends are important."

"I said I don't want to talk about it. Did you not hear me?"

"Paul," Mom chided.

I pushed away my plate and rose from the table.

"I could invite him over for dinner," Mom suggested.

"What? Mom, do not invite Roby over for dinner. Do not."

I strode out of the kitchen and out of the house. First Natalia, now Mom? How could Mom think that my friendship with Roby was any of her business? What gave her the right to be such a ... such a fucking parent?

I'd stormed out of the house with my phone, but without earbuds. Dammit. I could still listen to music, but I'd have to hold the phone up to my ear, and I'd look stupid. Plus I could see Mrs. Yannopoulos walking her German shepherd a couple of yards ahead of me. Did I want her hearing $uicideboy$ or Ghostemane, even for the few moments it would take for me to pass her? She'd pinch up her face and make me feel scolded, so, no, I did not.

I forced myself to unclench my fists.

I inhaled and exhaled. Told myself I was okay. *You're fine,* I told myself. *Chill. The fuck. Out.*

I sent Mom a grudging text.

Sorry for being salty, I was out of line

Three gray dots appeared, went away, appeared again.

Whatever's going on between you and Roby, you can't take it out on me.

I know, my bad.
But you don't always need to push on things.
My business with Roby is my business.

I'm your mom. I care.

The fight left me. I texted her back.

Fair enough. I'm going to Roby's.
I'll be back eventually.

Good luck.
I love you, Paul.

Love you too

"Paul!" Roby's mom exclaimed when she opened the door. Her eyes got shiny. "Paul, it's good to see you. Come in. We've missed you!"

I stepped into the entry hall, and the distinctive Smalls family smell enveloped me.

"Can I hug you?" Roby's mom asked. "I'm going to hug you."

She hugged me. I gave her an awkward pat. She held me at arm's length and took me in. "My goodness. You are so tall!"

"That's me." I kicked at the carpet, then got over myself and gave her a wide smile. I'd missed Mrs. Smalls. I'd missed all the Smalls.

"Let me call Roby," Mrs. Smalls said. She turned toward the staircase. "Roby! Ro-by!"

"Isn't that the thing kids get in trouble for on TV shows?" I asked. "When the parent says, 'Go call your sister,' and the kid bellows, 'SISTER!'"

"It's the privilege of being a parent. One day you'll understand." Roby thudded down the stairs. "You too, Roby."

"Me too what?" Roby said. He eyed me warily, though he didn't look surprised at my presence. He'd probably heard me talking to his mom.

"Never mind," Roby's mom said. She touched the poof of hair captured at the top of Roby's head, his newly minted man bun. "I can't wrap my head around boys' hairstyles these days. I really can't."

"Gotta get with the times, Mrs. S," I said.

"Do I?" Mrs. Smalls asked. She started to touch my hair but didn't. Instead, she smiled and retreated.

When it was just the two of us, Roby folded his arms over his chest and regarded me. "Did Natalia dump your sorry ass? Is that why you're here?"

"Dude. Uncool," I said. "And no." I paused. "Why? Is that what you want to happen?"

"If I said yes, would you break up with her?"

"No."

"Well, there you go."

"Roby."

He half shrugged. "You've been a douche, you know."

Natalia hated it when people used that term as an insult. So did my mom. I started to say so, then realized that – guess what? – Natalia wasn't here. Neither was Mom.

I tried to regulate my breathing. I hated feeling out of sync with Roby. I hated the tangle of emotions churning in my gut.

"I have been a douche, you're right," I said. "I guess I was worried things would be weird."

"Yeah, well, you've been leaving me out in the cold. You and Natalia both."

I felt awash with shame. "Sorry, bruh."

He ducked his head and muttered something along the lines of not wanting to be left behind. I couldn't ask him to repeat himself or suggest he speak a little louder.

I said, "I'll do better."

Roby kept his head down. Several seconds passed before he said, "You really like her?"

"I do."

He nodded. More time passed. Eventually he said, "Wanna play *Mortal Kombat*?"

We played for hours on his 4K TV. I stayed for dinner – meat loaf and corn on the cob – and Roby farted. I'd missed Roby's enormous TV, and I'd missed Roby. I hadn't missed his farts. I recoiled and swatted the air.

"Now, Paul," Roby chided. "You are a guest at this table. Show some respect."

"Can't. No oxygen."

"Anyway, it's not me. It's the corn."

"You always blame the corn."

Roby's fart made its way around the table, and Mrs. Smalls wrinkled her nose.

"For the love of God, son," said Roby's dad.

"My mom makes him bring a bottle of Febreze when he spends the night," I said companionably.

"What?" Mrs. Smalls exclaimed.

"Yeah, yeah, fun times," Roby said, pushing his chair away from the table. "Mom, thanks for dinner. Paul, one last round of *MK5*?"

We played one last round. Then a second last round.

"One more?" Roby said.

I checked my watch and tossed my controller onto the coffee table. "I better go."

"I bet my mom can give you a ride home," Roby said. He craned his body sideways and yelled upstairs. "Mom! Can you give Paul a ride home, in like an hour?"

"Sure, honey!" Roby's mom called back. "Or he can sleep over if that works!"

Roby looked at me and raised his eyebrows.

I grabbed my controller and went samurai on his ass.

chapter twenty-two

In April of junior year, I finally did what I had to do to get my learner's license. Hold the applause, send gold instead. Or Gucci.

I sat through three endless Saturdays at Blue Ridge Mountain Driving School, learning traffic laws and watching videos about crash-test dummies getting brutally killed in fake accidents. After that, I took the road test with an instructor who communicated only with grunts.

Finally, Mom and I went to the DMV to turn in my paperwork. The woman behind the counter was young and pretty and wore lots of tinkling jewelry. Her name tag said THEA.

"This kid!" Mom said. "Can you believe he's only now getting his learner's? He turns seventeen next month! In May!"

"I think she knows the order of the months, Mom," I said.

"When you were a teenager, didn't you want to get your license right away?" Mom asked Thea. "I sure did."

"Everyone has their own timeline," Thea said, flashing me a conspiratorial smile.

I smiled back. I don't want to sound arrogant, but I could tell she found me attractive, even though she was in her twenties and I was just shy of seventeen.

While Mom counted out bills and chatted with a second clerk, Thea leaned toward me and placed her hand on top of mine.

"Don't stress about being a new driver," she said in a soft voice. "It's intense. I get that." She leaned closer, her blouse falling open to reveal a lace bra and the tops of her tits. I glimpsed the pink tip of one nipple and got an immediate and intense erection.

Paul, buddy, pull it together, I told myself. I dragged my eyes to her face.

"Just take it at your own pace," Thea said.

"For sure," I said, battling a mix of lust and guilt.

I have a girlfriend, so I shouldn't think about other girls in that way. I never intend to think about other girls in that way, but sometimes it happens anyway. To be honest, it happens more often than not. Maybe this is wrong to say, but the physical reality of females is, like, inescapable. For me, that is. Breasts and asses – I can't *not* notice them. Same goes for smiles, for eyes, for pretty hands.

Natalia is more than a girl who happens to be beautiful, although she is beautiful. The beautiful-est. I see other girls, and yeah I feel desire or whatever. But that's all I feel. With Natalia, there's like this energy that hovers between us. Everything she has to say, I want to hear. She's funny, and she thinks I'm funny, which I am, but not everybody gets my sense of humor the way she does.

I even love hanging out with Natalia when her little sister is around and refuses to go away, because Lena is sweet and cute and hugs me super tight. Lena's favorite thing is to make us play Candy Land, and as long as I can touch Natalia while we play, like with my foot on hers or her hand on my thigh, I'm good. That's saying a lot. Candy Land is boring as fuck.

And yet ... Thea, this DMV lady who was flirting with

me. Girls I see at school, girls I see at the grocery, girls I see on TV shows.

Maybe my raging hormones will calm down once Natalia and I have sex. I hope so.

Two weeks ago Natalia went to Planned Parenthood. She went on her own, without telling me, and got a prescription for birth control pills. She told me that for Catholics, which she was, abortion was a worse sin than sex.

"Is sex a sin?" I asked.

"With you?"

"Of course with me!" I didn't want to think about her having sex with some other guy, ever.

"Technically, yes, but I'm not planning to wait till I'm married," Natalia said in her soft voice that's so much sexier than Thea's. Natalia is sexier than Thea in every way, her tits especially. And her lips. And her ass. Natalia has this one pair of shorts and, damn. When she walks, they ride up so high I can see the fold between her thighs and her ass cheeks.

Sometimes I toss Natalia over my shoulder and carry her around the room, her butt in the air as she laughs and kicks. I like being strong enough to do that. I like that she's so much smaller than me, with cute small girl muscles. Natalia digs it, too. She likes to trace the line of my jaw, then stroke my lower lip with her thumb. She likes to wrap both hands around my biceps, and she gives me the most adorable look when she can't get her fingertips to touch.

"Strong boy," she whispers.

"Smart girl," I reply. "Sexy girl."

Mom offered to let me drive home from the DMV with my newly minted learner's license. I said, "Nah," and strode out of the building without a backward glance.

I'm sure I'll like driving one day, but right now the pros don't outweigh the cons.

chapter twenty-three

Natalia and I had sex.

Natalia and I. Had. Sex.

Holy shit, I'm no longer a virgin. Natalia is no longer a virgin. Neither of us will be virgins ever again.

I sprawled next to Natalia on her bed, both of us sweaty and happy and naked except for one lone sock dangling from my left foot. I'd peeled the other sock off earlier, and tried to use my bare foot to push off its mate, but I'd gotten involved in other things. Now and forever I'd be the guy who had sex for the first time with half a sock on, and you know what? I was okay with that.

More than okay.

I rolled onto my side and grazed my knuckles over Natalia's cheek. "You are amazing."

She smiled.

I slid my arm beneath her, drawing her close until her head rested on my chest. With her finger, she drew loops on my skin. Her body was warm against mine, and silky smooth, and it blew my mind to think that I'd been inside her only moments ago. My dick had grown stiff and big, and I'd nudged apart her legs with my knee and pushed myself into her.

Warm and wet. Tight and soft. Warm and wet and soft.

I got hard again.

"Paul!" Natalia whispered, finding and stroking the length of me. I rolled over and pinned her beneath me. She squeaked. I cupped one breast and sucked her nipple. Her squeak turned into something else.

"God, I love you," I said.

"And I love you," she said. She made a sound of pleasure, and my dick pulsed with needing her.

"Again?"

"Again."

We did, again and again.

senior

year

chapter
twenty-four

Senior year was a lot like junior year, only with more parties. When I wasn't with Natalia, I was with my guy friends. Mainly I hung out with Roby and Monty, although other guys drifted in and out of our group. Every weekend someone's parents went out of town, freeing a house for the evening's festivities. Someone always managed to score a keg or weed or coke, or all three. One night some dude's cousin showed up with fentanyl, but I was all, "Nah, I'm good." I'm up for most things, but the possibility of overdosing on horse sedatives held no appeal.

Tonight was the last Saturday of October, and Roby

and I were having a chill night at Monty's house. Like me, Monty lives with just his mom. In middle school we didn't spend much time together. Now we hang out regularly.

"Whoa," Monty said, considering me from a hammock chair that nearly swallowed him. His eyes were half-lidded. He held a blunt between his thumb and his forefinger. "Paul Walden, in the flesh."

Roby raised his eyebrows. "You actually showed, big man."

He was ragging on me for the times I hadn't, because for whatever reason I was off with Natalia. Roby gives me grief about her, and she gives me grief about him. It's a pain in the ass.

I relieved Monty of the blunt and finished it off, holding the smoke nice and tight before slowly exhaling.

Natalia, for the record, only smokes once in a blue moon, and when she does, she takes super-shallow puffs. She says weed "doesn't work with her body chemistry." I say, "Give it time. I think you'd really love it if you got used to it." She says, "Paul, why would I want to get used to it?"

Whatever. I'm not going to be peer pressure-y about it.

She called while I was playing *Fortnite* with the boys.

"Hold on," I said as I snaked my way through outstretched legs and over an impressive collection of Coke cans, beer cans, and crumpled chip bags. Monty's mom either didn't actually exist or never came down to the basement.

"Kissy, kissy!" Monty called over his shoulder.

I shot him the bird.

"What's up?" I said when I was far enough away to talk.

"Where are you?" Natalia asked. She sounded pissed, and I racked my brain. Had I forgotten something? Some obscure nine-month-and-nine-days anniversary? Natalia kept track of that stuff. She even knew the exact day we first kissed. She called it our "kissiversary," and she marked it on her calendar with a tiny red heart.

"At Monty's," I said. "Everything cool?"

"Seriously, Paul?" she said. "You're seriously asking that?"

I gripped my phone. "Natalia, are you okay?"

"No, I'm upset. Where are you?"

"I already told you, I'm —"

"Let me rephrase. Why aren't you here?"

Here where? Where was here?

"At the Music Center," Natalia said icily. "*The Sound of Music*? Kahlia is playing Liesl?"

I pressed the heel of my palm to my forehead. The Music Center is an internationally known performing arts center in Brevard. They draw Grammy-winning musicians as well as top-dog performers, and Kahlia, a local, had scored a role in this season's musical. Tonight's performance was the last of the season.

I'm not big into musicals, but I'd promised Natalia I'd be there. She bought a new dress, and I'd planned to wear my finest swag so we'd match. Khaki joggers paired with a Burberry button-down I bought on Grailed, finished off with Thom Browne dress shoes that one of Mom's clients had passed along because they were too tight for her husband. If I'd bought the shoes new, they would have cost nine hundred and fifty dollars. I looked it up.

But so, yeah. A romantic evening with my girlfriend, that had been the plan. Instead, I was hanging my head at Monty's house while Natalia guilt-tripped at me over the phone.

"Well?" Natalia demanded.

"Well, what?" I said reflexively.

Natalia huffed. I'd missed what she'd said, or multiple things she'd said. "Never mind."

"No, Natalia, wait."

"Tell her to quit her bitching!" Monty called. "You're holding up the game!"

"Who was that?" Natalia said. "Was that Monty? What did he say?"

"He wasn't talking about you."

"Bullshit."

"Natalia, listen," I said. "I'm dressed and ready. I'm just running late."

She didn't respond.

"I didn't forget. Did you really think I would forget? I lost track of time, that's all."

"You're wearing your nice clothes?"

"Of course. Your boy is dope."

She made a sound that told me she was relenting. "Well, hurry. The curtain goes up at seven."

I persuaded Mom to pick me up from Monty's. She was salty about it, but she came. She swung me by the house, and I threw on my nice clothes, gargled with mouthwash, and sprayed myself with cologne. I made it to the Music Center by a quarter past seven, but the ushers in their gray suits said I couldn't go to my seat until intermission.

Anger sparked from Natalia when I found her at the snack bar almost an hour later. She marched back to our seats. I followed meekly.

"You missed the entire first act," she whispered. She pressed her body against the side of her seat to keep from touching me.

"I screwed up," I whispered, "and I'm sorry. Will you please accept my apology?"

"And you missed Liesl's duet!"

I felt like an ass. "I am extremely sorry. Will you please accept my apology?"

The man in front of us turned and glared, but he was wearing a monocle, so it was hard to take him seriously.

"'Sixteen Going on Seventeen'?" Natalia hissed. "What about that?"

"Huh?"

Her mouth fell open.

"The song!" I said. "You're talking about the song. I totally knew that." I pretended to bash my head. "I am scum. I am a poop stain on a poop stain. Please, please, please accept my apology."

Monocle man glared. His wife turned and addressed Natalia, whispering, "Accept his apology, dear. For all our sakes."

"Fine," Natalia said, but she still didn't soften up and touch me until the musical was over and she gave me a ride home. When she pulled up in front of my house, I reached over and turned the ignition off.

"You smell amazing," I said. "And I really like your new dress."

"Hmm," she said.

Her dress had spaghetti straps. I slipped one strap down and caressed her shoulder. She pulled the strap back up and pushed away my hand.

"Paul," she said.

"Natalia," I said.

I slid my thumb under the ruffly top of her sundress. "No bra. I like."

"It's called fashion," she said. I grazed her nipple with my thumb. It stiffened, while the rest of her body grew softer and more pliant.

"Goddammit, Paul," she murmured.

"I really am sorry about being late tonight," I said. "I don't ever want to do something that makes you sad."

"Well, you did."

"I'll learn from it. I swear." I paused. "I love you, Natalia." She arched her neck, and I kissed the hollow between her collarbones. "So all is forgiven?"

She unfastened her seat belt and wiggled over the console to straddle me, her sundress hiking up.

The strap over her shoulder was slack, so I tugged on it. Her dress slid down and gathered around her waist.

Her breasts. So perfect.

She put one hand behind my neck and the other on my dick.

"Natalia," I groaned.

"I love you, too," she whispered, her lips brushing mine. "But sometimes..."

I nuzzled the skin behind her ear. "Yes?"

"Sometimes, I think I have to say no."

"To me? To sex? Natalia, what are you saying?"

"Just, would you work on remembering that there are other people in the world besides you?"

I totally remembered that there were other people in the world besides me. There was Natalia, who was on my lap, whose breasts were in my face. I moved to take her nipple in my mouth.

She moved her hand from my dick to my chest, pushing gently to create space between us. "You're sweet, and you're funny. You're insanely gorgeous."

"Not as gorgeous as you."

She didn't smile, and my stomach flipped. She did know how desperately I loved her, didn't she? Even if I messed up sometimes?

"But Paul, you hurt people – me – without meaning to," she said. "Not always. Not usually. But when you do, I feel so stupid. Like sloppy seconds."

I didn't even know what that expression meant. Still, heat rushed to my face. I fought not to get angry, not to cry.

Natalia pulled up her dress. She wiggled the shoulder straps back into place.

"Things matter," she said. "What we do. How we treat each other. You think it's just a game, I think."

"I don't."

"But it's *life*," she said. "This ... Paul ... this is what life *is*."

She opened the passenger door and climbed out of her car, waiting on the street until I got out after her.

"Good night?" I said.

She placed her palm on my cheek. She kissed me. Then she walked to the opposite side of the car, slid into the driver's seat, and turned on the engine.

"All is *almost* forgiven," she called as she pulled away. "Keep working on it."

chapter twenty-five

Natalia, Kahlia, and Helen are always saying "Love you!" to each other. They say it at school, at parties, at each other's houses. They hug all the frickin' time, too. Guys, on the other hand, bump fists, and every so often hug their moms.

Still, Roby's my best bud, and I don't need to hug him to prove it. That's what I was thinking about a couple of weeks after my fight with Natalia – although, to be fair, *fight* is too strong a word. There'd been tension between us, and it had felt big during the moment, but it passed.

But see, that's what's great about guy friends. No drama, no "talks," hardly ever any tension.

Tonight, a dozen seniors were hanging out at a guy named Harry's house, and I grinned as I watched Roby sip his Corona. He'd been nursing that one beer all night, because he was the designated driver for me and two other guys. He'd brought a lime in the pocket of his jacket, which he washed and cut when we arrived. Then he ran a slice around the rim of his Corona bottle and pushed that sucker in.

"Is that slice of lime your comfort animal?" I asked.

"What are you talking about?" he said.

"Your blankie. Your security thingie."

Roby patted my head. "Nope. My lime is classy, and you know why? Because I'm classy."

Half an hour later, Roby abandoned his half-finished Corona to play hero, because Lily was so wasted she couldn't walk straight. Lily from freshman year, from Stevie and the sex slaves, although she's changed a lot since then. These days she's best friends with Gertrude Leibowitz. They're both into activism and are always going on marches and shit.

I don't know what Lily's deal was tonight, if she had a fight with her boyfriend or if it was something else, but out of nowhere she was all, "I have to go home. I have to go home!"

She snatched up her keys and stumbled through the crowd while her friends trailed behind her, saying stuff like, "Was it Brennen? What did he do?" and, "If he was with Cerise? Dude, I swear I'll kill him for you."

I told Lily that she was in no state to drive, but she pushed past me. She tried to get past Roby, too, but he blocked her on the driveway. Roby is a small man. Still, he's a guy, and has guy muscles, and when he grabbed Lily's shoulders, she couldn't twist away.

"Lily, you're not driving," he said. "Give me your keys."

"No. I have to go home!" Lily slurred.

"That's fine," Roby said, "but give me your keys."

Lily swayed. Roby held her up. "What about my car? I can't leave it here."

"I'll drive you," Roby said.

"But I don't know you," Lily wailed. "You could be a serial killer! Or a rapist!"

"I'm not. I promise. And I'm in your chemistry class."

She peered at him. "Are you? I don't think so. I think I would know who's in my own chemistry class."

"I'll drive you home, and you can go to your room and find last year's yearbook. Last year, we had environmental science together."

"Nope. No siree Bob." She angled her head and squinted. "Are you Bob? I don't know any Bobs except my uncle, and you are not my uncle, mister! Ha! Got you there!"

Roby kept one hand on her shoulder and wiggled the fingers of his other. "Keys?"

She made a toddler's sullen pout but dropped the keys into his palm.

"Great. You're doing great," Roby said. "Let's get you into your car, okay?"

Wrong move. Lily went from pout to tantrum, shaking her head so vigorously that strands of blond hair lashed her face. She teetered. "No taking rides from strangers. No, no, no."

Roby sighed. "Give me a sec. Can you give me a sec?"

"Yes, Uncle Bob." She blinked. "Gertrude, where are you? Ger-trude!"

Roby propped Lily against a tree. She slid down the trunk, and her camisole rode up, snagging on the bark.

"Owwww," she moaned. "Gertrude, I have tree burn! Gertrude, help!"

While Gertrude ministered to Lily's scratches, Roby interrogated Lily's other friends. "Are you good to drive? How much have you had to drink?" Then, to the next person, "Are *you* good to drive?"

"What about Paul?" Gertrude suggested. She stroked Lily's hair and pointed at me. "You know Paul, don't you, Lily?" she said in a don't-scare-the-tiny-animal voice. "He's Natalia's boyfriend."

Lily's head lolled onto Gertrude's shoulder. "You guys are sooooo cute," she said, aiming her remark in my general vicinity. "How long have you two been together? Are you going to get married and have babies?" She turned and pressed her forehead against Gertrude's forehead. "Wouldn't Paul and Natalia have the cutest babies?"

"The cutest," Gertrude agreed. "So you'll let Paul drive you home?"

I cleared my throat. "I can't. I don't have my license."

"You don't have it with you, or you don't have it at all?"

"At all."

Gertrude screwed up her face. "You still haven't gotten your license? Dude."

"Also, I've been drinking."

Roby approached me, jiggling Lily's keys. "Call Natalia," he said. "Ask her to come pick Lily up."

I groaned and said, "Roby, no." Natalia had turned down Harry's invitation, saying she needed to study for her chemistry test, and she'd urged me to do the same.

"Forget the party," she'd wheedled. "Come to my house and study with me."

Roby pulled up Natalia's number and pressed his phone into my hand. His contact picture of her, I saw, was from when we were sophomores. She was sitting on top of the monkey bars at Straus Elementary and laughing, her head tossed back and her dark hair gleaming.

Roby reached over and pressed call.

"Fuck," I said, raising the phone to my ear.

Natalia wasn't happy at being summoned. Still, she picked Lily up from Harry's house and drove her home. Roby and I followed in Lily's car. Natalia coasted to a stop half a block from Lily's house, and Roby pulled up behind her. He got Lily out of Natalia's car and helped her into the driver's seat of her own.

"Just pull into the driveway, turn off the car, and go inside," he instructed. "You can do that, right?"

Lily was still drunk, but slightly less so. She had raccoon eyes from her trashed mascara. "Yes, Dad."

"Don't forget to turn off the headlights. You don't want to drain the battery."

"Yes, Dad."

Natalia pulled me to the side. "You should have ridden with me, not Roby."

"Oh," I said. "Sorry."

Once Lily was safely inside her house, Roby asked Natalia to take us back to Harry's. Natalia raised her eyebrows at me. I pretended not to understand.

"I'm not saying drop us off," Roby said. He flexed his hand in a raise-the-roof movement. "Come with. You can watch Paul get lit. Yeah-uh!"

"I've got better things to do," Natalia said.

"Like what, homework? On a Friday night?"

"Yes, actually," Natalia said.

"All right. Respect," Roby said.

She agreed to drive Roby back to Harry's, though. I climbed into the front with her, while Roby clambered into the back seat and blared Yung Pinch on his phone. He sang along, bobbing his head. *Yeah, all the girls gonna flock to this, don't matter where you from, you could rock with us!*

At Harry's house, I stayed in Natalia's car and told Roby to go in without me.

Roby stood on the street and leaned into the open passenger seat window. The lights from the party illuminated his man bun, and I could make out the loose strands that were trying to make a break for it.

"Tell me you're kidding," he said. He saw my expression, and his face fell. "Really? But Paul. We rescued Lily. We did it together."

I nodded. I felt good about that part of the evening, but bad about dragging Natalia into it. By this point, returning to the party felt more like a chore than something fun. But then, so did leaving with Natalia, especially with Roby standing witness. I couldn't win for losing.

"Fine, fine," Roby said, lifting his hand as he headed toward the house. I watched him go. Then I decided, *No.* This wasn't how I wanted the night to end. As Natalia herself said, I wasn't the only person in the world. Roby, he was a person in the world, too. I'd come to this party with him, and I'd leave with him.

I climbed out of the car and walked to the driver's side. Natalia stuck her head out the window and said, "Paul...?"

I leaned down and said, "Cut me some slack, all right?"

Natalia didn't say anything. She just pressed her lips together and drove off.

I stayed outside for several minutes, linking my hands around the back of my neck and gazing at the stars. Being forced to divide my time between my girlfriend and my best friend wasn't the worst problem in the world, I supposed, since it was a problem that hinged on having both a girlfriend *and* a best friend. It was what Mom would call a champagne problem. It was what I might call ... I don't know. A Pabst Blue Ribbon problem?

I found Roby standing guard outside the closed door of the sole bathroom in Harry's small house. He stood with his feet spread and his arms folded over his chest.

"Hey, man," I said.

"Paul!" he said. "You came back!"

I popped open a fresh beer. "What are you doing? You look like a bouncer."

"Gertrude's in there. Now *she's* drunk as fuck."

"Sucks. Is she barfing?"

"She's taking a bath."

"I'm sorry, what?"

"She's drunk and naked and taking a bath," Roby said. "She's watching shows on her iPad. *Orange Is the New Black.*"

"What if she drowns?"

"She's not that drunk."

"What happens when people need to take a piss?"

I asked, and by virtue of posing the question, I promptly needed to do just that.

"Gotta go outside, guy," Roby said. "Tree pee."

"What about the girls?"

Roby rapped on the bathroom door. "Gertrude, you okay with girls using the bathroom if they need to?"

"I'm taking a bath!" she called indignantly.

"Yeah, Roby," I said. "She's taking a bath, you nut."

There's a movie Roby and I love called *Die Hard*, where Bruce Willis plays a cop named John McClane who rescues all these hostages from a group of terrorists. McClane is trapped with the terrorists on the thirtieth floor of a skyscraper, and the way he keeps track of what's going on in the world beyond the skyscraper – like with the FBI and the police and the media vans – is by communicating via walkie-talkie with an LAPD desk officer named Al. Al's overweight and has a great smile and gives these loud belly laughs when something funny happens. But when serious things happen, which is most of the movie, Al is serious and on the ball. When Bruce Willis saves everyone, it's in large part thanks to Al.

At the end of *Die Hard*, John McClane stumbles out of the skyscraper all bloody and sweaty. He locks eyes with his new buddy, Al. It's the first time McClane sees Al in the flesh, and the same goes for Al with McClane, but even so they recognize each other. McClane clasps Al in a hug, and Al slaps McClane's back. Neither of them says a word, although Al smiles and nods when they draw apart, as if to say, *Good job, man. Nice work.*

Roby was my Al – or hell, I was *his* Al, and he was my John McClane. Because that night at Harry's house, Gertrude stayed in the tub for over an hour. Roby guarded the door, and I kept him company. No one barged in, not to pee, not to take a shit, not to cop a look at a naked girl taking a bath and watching Netflix.

"Roby, buddy, I am proud to call you my friend," I told him, probably around midnight.

"You still have to pee outside," Roby said.

"Who said I need to pee?"

He looked at me.

"All right, fine," I said. I raised my half-empty beer. "You'll be here when I return?"

"Always," he said.

Yippee ki-yay, motherfucker.

chapter
twenty-six

On a Sunday in early November, Mom asked if I wanted to go driving with her, rack up some hours for my practice log.

I begged off, telling her I had an essay to write. "It's due tomorrow," I said truthfully. "I have to say what my 'ideal lifestyle' is."

"Your ideal lifestyle," Mom repeated. "Are you sure you'll be able to articulate your ideal lifestyle in one afternoon?"

"I am not, but I'm willing to try."

In my room, I opened my laptop and typed "My Ideal Lifestyle" in the center of page one.

One line below, I typed "by Paul Walden." Six words down! Yeah!

An hour later, it was done. I'm not saying it was good, but it was done, and it wasn't even three o'clock.

My phone buzzed. I checked the screen and took the call. "Yo, Roby. 'Sup?"

"Monty and I are coming to get you," Roby said.

"Oh, yeah? What's the plan?"

"No plan, just looking for fun. Monty has to clean his room —"

"For real? That boy never cleans his room."

"But as soon as he's done, I'll pick him up, and then we're heading your way."

He hung up, and I wandered off in search of Mom. I found her in the laundry room.

"Roby and Monty want to hang out," I told her. "Is that cool?"

"Have you finished your homework?" Mom asked.

"I have."

"Wow."

"Indeed."

"Then, sure." She craned her neck to gaze up at me. "You are so tall," she marveled. It was true. I'd grown another inch, bringing me to six feet two.

"You're so small," I countered. I slung my arm around her and kissed the top of her head.

I sat on the front porch to wait for Roby and Monty. It was chilly out, but I found a spot of sunshine and tilted my face to soak up the rays. As I sat there, my back against the wall, I grew super crazy drowsy, the kind of drowsiness where I literally have to slap and pinch myself to stay awake.

I dug out my phone. "Hey, Roby, are you close?"

"I'm still at my house," he said. "Monty's being slow."

"I'm fading, bro. I'm afraid I might fall asleep."

"I'll bring those chubby cashews you love. Snack food for the win."

"Dude, those cashews are lit. Only I seriously might fall asleep."

"Drink a Red Bull."

"Can't. My mom won't let me have them in the house."

"Then drink a Coke. Drink two Cokes."

"Will do. Just, I might fall asleep anyway. You know how it goes."

"You're killing me, bruh," Roby said.

"I'll try to stay awake. Just get here soon."

Mom glanced up as I passed back through the house. "Did you change your mind?"

"Nah, Roby's not here yet. I'm going to wait in the basement."

"Come give me a hug before you go downstairs," she said.

I obliged, and she squeezed my waist. "You're a good son, Son."

"You're a good mama, Mama," I said. I blinked my way to my room and crashed.

chapter
twenty-seven

My phone buzzed, pulling me out of a deep, dreamless sleep. It was Monty.

"I was in the car," he said.

I blinked and pushed myself to sitting. It was five o'clock. I'd missed three calls from Roby. *Shit.* I also had over a hundred Snapchat notifications. What the hell?

Right. Would deal with that later. Dragging my hand down my face, I said, "Monty. Hey."

"I was in the car," he repeated.

"Dude. What car?"

"Have you checked Snapchat? Don't. You shouldn't find out that way. No one should."

"Find out what?"

"We were just driving, man. We went down Wilson Road, out near Connestee Falls." His sentences tumbled over each other. "It was sunny. It was a nice day, a really nice day, you know?"

"Monty, for real, what are you going on about?"

"We came to pick you up. Your mom tried to wake you."

I took in all the crap littered across my floor. I hoped she'd knocked on my door and nothing else.

"Roby had the windows down and the heater going full blast," Monty said. "Only he hogged the heat, pointing the vents just on him." Monty laughed, but it wasn't a normal laugh.

Someone squeezed an invisible hand around my lungs.

"He was just fooling around. He didn't ... we didn't..." Monty sucked in air. "It's fine that he hogged the heat! I'm glad he hogged the heat!"

"Where are you?" I asked. "Where's Roby?"

"We were bumping hard, singing along at the top of our lungs. I'm telling you, it was the perfect day. The perfect everything!"

My mouth was dry. I had to work my tongue around

before I could speak. "Put Roby on the phone. Okay, Monty?"

Monty puked. That's what I thought at first.

"Dude... Monty..."

He wasn't puking. He was wailing. He unleashed a flood of sobs that came and came and wouldn't stop.

"What happened?" I managed as my muscles turned to water. "Was there an accident? Were you in a wreck?"

Monty spoke in spurts. I recognized the words, and knew them, and yet they passed through my brain like clouds scuttling across the sky.

Roby wasn't speeding, Monty said. He was being totally safe, like always, and yes, they both wore their fucking seat belts. They were on the straight stretch of road along the pasture. There were no other cars in sight, although there were cows in the fields. They lifted their heads as Roby drove by.

He hit a bump, Monty said. He lost control, and the car slammed into a tractor parked on the side of the road. And then Monty's words became fragments of glass, broken and glittering, but it didn't matter, because I wasn't there. I was distant and far away. I'd been lifted out of my body.

"His seat belt —"

"Monty. Stop."

"The EMTs, they said —"

"Shut up, Monty. Shut up, shut up, shut up."

The car hood crumbled. Monty scratched his wrist. Roby's seat belt locked when he slammed on the brakes, and he broke his neck.

"The EMTs said he would have died instantly," Monty managed. "No pain. But Paul..." His breath hitched, and he lost himself to another bout of sobs. "I saw him, Paul."

"I don't want to hear it," I said. But I saw him, too. Not then, but later, in my relentless and unforgiving imagination: Roby's broken neck. The angle of his head. Blood and skin and bone.

He died.

Roby died.

The sun went down. The sun came up.

I breathed against my will. With every breath, Roby died again.

chapter
twenty-eight

I keep thinking the story will change, that I'll wake up and everything will make sense again.

Like, I don't want this truth either, but if Roby pushed a kid out of the way of a train or rescued a baby from a burning building?

If he saved an old lady from a rabid dog.

If he saved an old lady from a rabid gerbil.

It still wouldn't make sense, but it would make more sense.

Monty got a scratch on his wrist.

My heart no longer lives in my body.

chapter twenty-nine

I told Mom that I was supposed to have been with them in the car. I sat beside her on the sofa the day after it happened and told her I'd said yes to driving around, but then I'd gone and fallen asleep.

"I took a nap," I said. "A nap!" My eyes were puffy and sore, and it hurt to rub them. So I rubbed them harder.

"Baby," said Mom, who had yet to stop crying.

I couldn't look her in the eye, so I gazed at her neck, at the small gold cross that nestled in the hollow of her throat. "Why, Mom?" What I meant was, *Why did it happen? Why can't you fix it? Why can't I? Why did I fall asleep, and why didn't you wake me?*

If I'd gone with them. If I hadn't fallen asleep. If I'd fallen asleep, but then woken up when Mom knocked on my bedroom door. Maybe Roby would have hit the bump earlier or later, or not at all. Maybe I would have been riding shotgun instead of Monty, and maybe I'd have seen the bump and called out to Roby, or grabbed the wheel myself.

"Oh, baby," Mom said. She drew me toward her and let me lie in her lap, like I did when I was little. I rolled onto my side and drew my knees toward my chest, tucking my hands under my chin. She ran her fingers through my hair.

"I don't think there is a 'why,'" she said.

"But it's so stupid. There's absolutely no reason Roby had to die."

"I know."

"No, Mom, you're not listening. People don't just up and die with no warning! It's ... they're there one day and gone the next? Just gone?"

"I know. It doesn't seem fair."

"Because it isn't! Roby was seventeen! He was my age!"

"What happened was an accident, a terrible, tragic accident," Mom said. "But, Paul, even with what happened with the seat belt, that doesn't mean seat belts aren't —"

"Don't," I said, fury coiling beneath my skin.

Her hand stilled on my hair. I held myself rigid and breathed as shallowly as I could. "Nothing I say is going to make things any better," Mom said. "There might not be answers. There might not be reasons. Accidents sometimes happen, and when they do..."

Her words went nowhere.

"Then what's the point?" I said. "What's the point of any of it?"

Mom kissed my forehead, then my temple, then my wet cheek. When she spoke, there was a quiver in her voice. "My sweet boy, I love you with every single bit of me."

She wrapped her arms around me and rocked me like a baby.

chapter thirty

Just kidding, Roby didn't die. The world played a horrible joke on me, and so I played a horrible joke on you and said that he did, but he didn't.
Because why would Roby die?
It makes no sense.
It makes
no
sense.

chapter
thirty-one

I met Roby in the men's room at the movie theater, both of us trying not to cry as we pissed side by side. Then he showed up in Ms. Summers's class, where we talked about lobsters and love and the difference between males and females.

When you're dead, there isn't a difference.

When you're dead, everyone's the same.

chapter thirty-two

Two nights after the accident, I asked Mom if I could please have a beer.

"I don't think that's a good idea," she said.

"All right," I said. "Can I have one anyway?"

Mom pressed her lips together, then gave a quick nod. "Yes, I suppose, but we don't have any beer. There's some gin in the liquor cabinet."

"Great. So I can help myself?"

She started to rise. "No. I'll get it for you."

"Please. Let me do it."

She sighed. "Only a little, Paul."

I turned on my heel. "Of course."

I don't remember everything that happened after that. I do remember thinking, *Fuck it,* and retreating to the basement with the Bombay Sapphire in hand. I drank it straight from the bottle, because why did it matter?

I must have fallen asleep, or maybe I passed out. At some point, my phone dinged, and I fumbled for it groggily. It took some serious blinking before I could decipher Mom's text.

Hey Paul. How much gin did you have? It seems like a lot is gone from the bottle.

I scanned my bedside table, my dresser, the floor next to my bed. No bottle of Bombay Sapphire. Had I returned it to the liquor cabinet?

I must have. Wow, that was somewhat impressive.

Just a little, like you said.

I think you had more than that, baby.

I might have I'm very sorry
It didn't seem like a lot at the time
but sounds like I screwed up

I'm not mad. I just want you to be safe.

I'm sorry if I poured too much,
I didn't know it was such a high
percentage of alcohol

**Okay, well, when you drink too much without
being aware of it, it's dangerous.**

Trust me I'm fully aware
That's why I stopped and put it away
I'm going to bed now, I'm sorry again
that I poured too much

Three dots appeared, disappeared, appeared. At last came Mom's message:

Get some rest, sweetheart.

Oh, man, I thought. Half laughing, I opened Snapchat to tell Roby what a dumbshit I was, and —
Goddammit.
I flung my phone across the room.

chapter
thirty-three

When I was little, before Mom and Dad got divorced, we had a housekeeper who came to our house three days a week. Her name was Shonda, and I loved her lots. She loved me too, which I know because she told me so, all the time. She made my chocolate milk with just the right amount of Ghirardelli cocoa (post-divorce, we switched to Nesquik), and she served it ice-cold in a tall glass.

Shonda died when I was in the third grade, and Dad paid for her funeral, because otherwise she would have had a "pauper's burial." That's what Dad said. For a long time I guess I thought pauper's burials weren't a real thing, until my eighth-grade music teacher made our class watch a movie about Mozart, who ended up dying a beggar even though he was a genius.

In the movie, Mozart's corpse was tossed into a cart on top of five or six other corpses, and then those corpses were dumped into a pit along with a bunch more corpses. Then the workers poured lye over them.

Once a soul has left a body, the body is just a shell. I get that. Mozart's dead body was no longer Mozart. Shonda's dead body was no longer Shonda. Even so, I'm glad Dad made sure Shonda was buried in a proper grave.

At Shonda's funeral, before the preacher talked, everyone formed a line to walk past Shonda's open casket. As we shuffled forward, I squeezed Mom's hand.

"You don't have to look," Mom whispered. "Just keep your eyes down, if that makes you feel better."

Except dropping my gaze felt disrespectful. I felt a huge weight to "do the right thing," even though it frightened me.

When it was our turn to pay our respects, the preacher said, "You must be Paul. I've heard so much about you."

My throat tightened.

"You were very special to her, young man," he said.

Shonda's hands were folded over her chest. I reached out to her, not thinking, and my fingertips grazed her cold skin. Then Dad's hand was on my shoulder, pulling me into a hug. "I've got you, buddy," he said, his breath warm against my ear. "You're safe."

I'd been frightened and confused – and then, because of Dad, the world tilted back into place. He was strong. He was big. His assurance washed over me like ... I don't know, the best security blanket ever.

On the day of Roby's funeral, Dad drove to Brevard to attend the service, but I no longer knew him the way I once did. Then again, I no longer knew anyone the way I once did. On the day of Roby's funeral, everyone seemed like a stranger.

Mom and Dad sat at the front of the church, with Roby's parents.

I sat in the back with Natalia and Gertrude and other kids from our grade. Gertrude looked devastated. Kahlia clutched Natalia's hand and cried.

Stevie Hardman was there. He looked like a zombie.

Monty didn't sit with us, because Monty didn't come.

Nobody had me. I wasn't safe. And that's all I have to say about Roby's funeral.

chapter thirty-four

When we got home, I paced in circles around the kitchen. I wanted to punch the wall. I wanted to kick the door frame. I wanted to take all the feelings inside me and wad them up and set them on fire. I wanted to set myself on fire.

I spotted my Bathing Ape bucket hat on the granite island, and self-disgust flared within me. That morning, before the funeral, I'd come upstairs from my room wearing dress pants that were too small, a button-down that was too big, and my Bathing Ape bucket hat. When Mom saw me, she'd pressed her hand to her mouth and said, "Oh, honey."

"What?" I'd said. Had I tied my tie wrong? Missed a button on my dress shirt?

"Just ... oh, sweetheart," Mom said. "You can't wear a hat to church."

"Are you kidding me?" I blurted. "What the fuck, Mom! Are you fucking kidding me?"

But I'd ripped off my hat, crumpled it in my hand, and flung it onto the island.

Now I picked it up and searched for matches. I needed matches.

"Paul?" Mom said from the opposite side of the room.

I glared at her, because I knew what she doing. She was refusing to let me be in the kitchen alone, while at the same time staying out of my way as best she could. Why? Because I was raging. I was unpredictable. I was six feet two and coursing with testosterone. Maybe I'd set her on fire.

I kicked the wooden molding at the base of the island. It hurt like hell, so I did it again.

"Paul?" Mom said, in a horrible, careful, beware-of-the-teenager voice.

"Where are the matches?"

Her lips parted.

"Mom. Where are the fucking matches?"

She walked over and held out her hand. "Baby, give me your hat."

"What? No."

"Paul-o, you're not going to burn your hat. I'm not going to let you."

"Who says you get to let me? Who says you get to let me do anything?"

Mom tried to touch me. I twisted away. Snot and tears flowed everywhere.

"If Roby wanted to burn his stupid fucking hat ..." I swallowed. "If Roby was here, and he wanted to burn his stupid fucking hat, what do you think his mom would say? Huh, Mom? I bet Roby's mom would let him burn every fucking hat in the world! I bet she'd be overjoyed to let him burn his fucking hats!"

My tears were loud and ugly. Mom's were silent. She said again, "Oh, honey."

"I want to burn everything, Mom! I do!" I pounded the island with my fist. "It's all so stupid! My swag? My showpieces?"

She placed her hand on my back so very gently, like a butterfly. I sobbed, and she rubbed my back, moving her hand in small circles. I turned despite myself. I let her embrace me.

"Paul," she said. "Baby." She said those words, and she said others, like "hush now" and "shhh."

We sat, again, on the sofa. I put my head, again, in her lap. I sobbed for hours and years.

"Do you remember when you were three, and you choked on the Mento?" Mom asked.

I took a shuddering breath. Of course I did.

"There's a part of that story I never told you." She stroked my hair. "I'm going to tell you now, and your only job is to listen. Okay?"

I sniffled. I nodded.

"It was a Monday," Mom said. "You went to morning preschool, and I picked you up at noon. I was hoping you'd take a nap when we got home, because I was sad. That's what I was thinking about before I gave you the Mento, that I hoped you'd take a nap. Because right then, I didn't feel very much like being a mom."

"How come?"

"Do you remember Willow?"

My mind went blank. Then — oh. Willow, my little sister who never was, who died when Mom was seven months pregnant.

"A week before the Mento day, I gave birth to Willow," Mom said. "Except not birth, since Willow wasn't alive." She explained how she'd found out that Willow's heart had stopped beating. One week earlier, the doctor told Mom how healthy and strong Willow was, and then the next week, Willow was dead. No rhyme or reason. She died inside Mom's uterus, and Mom hadn't even known.

Mom had to deliver Willow anyway. She told me it hurt like hell, only unlike a normal delivery, there was no reward at the end. Just a dead baby. She told me that the nurse clucked when she saw Willow's body, saying, "Oh, look at her sweet club feet."

"I hated her for that," Mom said. "My daughter was dead, and the nurse thought it was the perfect time to point out my dead daughter's flaws."

She told me that she held Willow for several hours, before giving her, wrapped in a pink blanket, to that same nurse.

"What about Dad?" I asked. "Did he hold her?"

"Your dad was great through everything," she said softly. "But, no. He didn't."

Mom was still grieving Willow's death a week later, the day I choked on the Mento. Her milk had come in and was leaking everywhere. Every part of her hurt. All she wanted to do was sleep.

"And then I almost lost you," she said.

I pushed myself to a sitting position. She took my hands. "You were choking, and at first I couldn't do anything to help you. I thought, 'This is it. I'm going to watch my son die, right here and now.'"

"But you didn't," I said. "You got me out of my car seat and turned me upside down, and finally the Mento came out."

"And you picked it up and tried to eat it again," Mom said.

I choke-laughed.

"Later, once we were home and I knew you were safe, I called my mom," Mom went on.

"Grandmommy."

"Yes, Grandmommy. I told her what happened, and I said, 'I guess the universe was telling me to be grateful for the child I had and to stop wishing for more.'" Mom studied me. "Do you know what Grandmom said?"

I shook my head.

"She said, 'No, Callie, I think it's the universe telling you not to give Mentos to a toddler.'"

I dragged my hand under my nose.

Mom half smiled. "But you were all right. I was all right. And over time, I healed." She tucked my hair behind my ear. "And having you be there, having no choice but to get up and function in order to take care of you, it made all the difference in the world. You are my best boy. The child of my heart."

I welled up with fresh tears. Roby was his mom's best boy, the child of her heart. Only Roby was gone. Mrs. Smalls could look for him from now until the end of time, we could all look for him from now until the end of time, but he would never be found.

chapter thirty-five

I refused to get my driver's license. I refused to rack up the requisite number of hours, and Natalia gave me advice I neither asked for nor wanted.

"I know you're thinking about Roby," she said. "Not getting your license is, like, a gesture."

"No. I never wanted my stupid license."

"I think you don't want to drive since that's how Roby died. But Paul, Roby isn't here to appreciate the fact that you're holding yourself back for him."

"I'm not. I'm fucking scared, all right? I'm scared and sad and – forget it. Just fuck off," I told her. I'd been telling her that pretty much every day since Roby died.

This time, she gazed at me with a mixture of sorrow and frustration. She said, "Okay, you know what, Paul?"

"What?"

"You're mad at the world for moving on. You're mad at me for moving on."

"Wow," I said. "That's so great, how you know exactly what I'm feeling. That's so helpful, Natalia. Really. I mean it."

"Come find me when you want to be with me again," she said. "When you want to be present again. With me. Hopefully I'll still want that, too."

I knew I'd screwed up. But, hey, I'd screwed up so many times. "Natalia..."

She walked away, stretching her arm behind her and flashing her palm.

I told myself I was better off without her, which was a lie. I told myself she was better off without me, which was the truth.

Before Roby died, I smoked a lot of weed. I smoked weed to party. I smoked weed to relax. Only rarely did I dabble in pharmaceuticals, because – before Roby died – putting narcotics into my body seemed like a bad idea.

Like, weed is natural. Pills are made in labs.

You can't die from overdosing on weed. People overdose on opioids all the time. Back in the old days, pharmaceuticals seemed like too much risk for too little reward. Also, neither Natalia nor Roby was down for doing that stuff, so in a way they peer-pressured me into not doing it either.

But when Roby died, the seesaw fell out of balance, if that makes sense. Every day was a gray day. Every day hurt. I pretty much saw no way to move forward until I learned through experimentation that Xanax and other anti-anxiety meds do what they claim to do. Meaning, they work.

I didn't stop smoking weed. I'm sad and strung out, but I'm not crazy. I supplemented my weed habit with other drugs, that's all.

These days, anything's easy to come by. Pretty much every mom of every kid at Brevard High School has a prescription for xanny or Valium or Klonopin, and pretty much all of those moms' kids are happy to sell a pill or two for spare cash. I mean, I say that, but to be fair, I've never sold any of Mom's meds. I hope it never comes to that.

But it got to be a little much, buying pills one by one at school. The stress started to get to me, and that was ridiculous, worrying about how I'd buy my escape from worries.

My solution was to double down, buying xannies and Kpins from a guy I met at a party. His name's Charlie. Along with dealing, he works as a dishwasher at Quixote, and he has a starter mustache that makes me want to stick a strip of tape on top of it and rip it off. Charlie started off super sweet, super chill. I thought we were buds. But then I realized that our friendship has rules. He's the seller. I'm the buyer. He's still sweet and usually chill, but he's not my friend.

One night I came home mad faded, and Mom called me on it.

"You look rough," she said, intercepting me in the kitchen. "Where were you?"

"Out with friends," I said. "I told you."

"Where with friends? Were you at Monty's house?"

No, I was at Charlie's cramped apartment, where I traded a gold chain for product. "The Salty Porker Butt Hut and Grill," I said.

"Paul, that can't be a real place." She frowned. "That isn't a real place, is it?"

She couldn't even recognize a joke anymore. Damn. I was losing Mom just like I was losing everyone else.

"Fine," I said. "I was rolling with Lorenzo in a Benzo."

"Paul? You're scaring me."

Tiny mice scrabbled at my intestines. "It's a song, Ma. Cool it. And I don't appreciate being roasted as soon as I walk in the door."

"What?" Mom said. "How did I roast you?"

I took off my ball cap and pushed my fingers through my hair. I tugged it back on. "I'm tired, and I want to go to bed, and it hurts my feelings that you're being sus about me, all right?"

"*Sus?*"

"It means suspicious. God, Mom. It means you think I'm being shady when I'm not, and I would hope you would know better since I'm your son."

Tears welled in my eyes, and Mom's demeanor changed. "Oh, honey," she said, stepping closer and wrapping her arms around me. Awkwardly, I patted her back. She said, "Of course you're my son. I do know you."

No, she didn't, and no, I wasn't. Or maybe I was. What had she said?

"I'm super tired," I said. "Can I please go to bed?"

She nodded, and I looked away. I didn't want to see her concern.

Another time, I got lit in my bedroom and stumbled

to the kitchen for snacks, which I admit was a dumbass thing to do. But I was mother-fungry hungry. A boy has needs.

When I turned around from the pantry, there Mom was. "Are you eating Nesquik straight out of the container?" she asked.

I looked at my hands. In one was a spoon. In the other was the Nesquik. My mouth felt gritty. I swallowed, licked my lips, and dragged the back of my hand across my mouth.

"I prefer *tub*," I informed her.

"What?"

"Tub of Nesquik. Sheesh, Ma." I angled the Nesquik so that she could see the nutritional informations. Information? Fuck it, the chart with calcium and iron and shit. "Anyway, vitamins. I'm a growing boy."

Mom put her hands on her hips. "You already said that."

"I did?"

"You did. Are you high, Paul?"

"Mom. Mom, Mom, Mom."

"Are you?"

"Oh my god, Mom," I said. "It's possible I might have imbibed slightly, but don't worry. I'm a heavyweight."

For some reason there were now two of her, which was a clever trick on her end. Or maybe my eyes were broken? I held out my thumb and index finger and tried to pinch her back together.

"Paul? Saying you're a 'heavyweight' doesn't make me feel better at all," Mom said. She sounded genuinely pissed.

Adrenaline jolted me into temporary sobriety, and I said, "Mama. Ma. You're tripping, Mom." I said, "I swear to God, I'm fine."

I wasn't.

I listened to rappers sing about addiction, and I told myself to get a grip. To get a grip, I'd take a dab and chew another Kpin.

The weed wasn't going to kill me, and if I drank while I was high, I passed out. Which was good. Passing out was my body's way of saving me from drinking more and getting alcohol poisoning.

The Klonopin, though. That was the bitch. When I started with Kpin, two milligrams got me nice and zooted. Two months later, my tolerance was so high that my maintenance dose was eight milligrams a day.

My maintenance dose, meaning that's how much I needed just to function. To get from strung out to calm required more on top of that.

One night I took sixteen milligrams over the course of several hours. After tossing back the last tablet, I got crazy drowsy. Like, I couldn't for the life of me keep my eyes open. I headed for the bathroom, intending to make myself throw up, but I fell asleep on the way there. When I woke up a day later, my brain had turned into cotton candy.

I Googled benzo-burnt, which was defined as "the utterly crap state of waking up after taking too many benzodiazepines and feeling more nervous, paranoid, and freaked out than you ever did pre-benzos." The sample sentence read, "I'm so benzo-burnt that I'd rather slide down a giant cheese grater than feel like this. I'm never taking more than 2 mgs of Klonopin in a single sitting again."

Well, shit, I thought.

Roby would have helped me come up with a plan to get clean.

Roby would have made sure I never got this fucked to begin with.

When I was with him, I knew who I was. I was Roby's

best friend, and he was mine, and we loved each other and had fun together and were heroes together. Who was I without him?

I told myself to quit using benzos.

Myself said, "Good luck with that, guy," because I could have all kinds of good ideas in the daylight, but when I was sitting in my room in the dark, and everything sucked, and I knew everything sucked and also that nothing was going to change, I couldn't make myself care.

Like, everyone's a candle, right? Imagine seven billion candles, and they're all lit. They all have a tiny golden flame flickering at the top.

They're pretty, but one by one, they're going to go out. More candles will come along, but they'll go out, too. All the candles will go out, always. Mom says that nothing matters and therefore everything matters. I say nothing matters, and therefore nothing matters.

When I looked in the mirror, I was dead inside.

chapter
thirty-six

I've been thinking back to when I was younger, before I had a clue about benzos or purple drank or even weed. I was so innocent. As Mom would say, I was too young to realize how young I was. Then, when the scales fell from my eyes, I felt ashamed of how innocent I'd been, like I'd done something wrong just by being a dumbshit kid.

Now, I wish I could go back. I wish I could be that dumbshit kid again, naive and full of hope.

I was a good kid once upon a time. I really was. Like, when I was a freshman, I went to this kid Eli's house for a party. Roby was there, too. Eli and me and

Roby and four others. We played *Mortal Kombat,* and Eli used cheat codes that gave him infinite lives.

At nine forty-five, Eli's mom popped into the basement and said, "Eli, your father and I are heading to bed."

"Yep," Eli said, not looking away from the TV.

She smiled at me and Roby and the other guys. "Good night, boys. Lights off in an hour, all right?"

"Yes, ma'am," I said. "Thanks for having us."

"Good night, Mom," Eli said. He maintained his bland expression as his mom headed upstairs, then curled his lip. "They'll be conked by ten, and we can sneak out."

My muscles clenched up, because I wasn't a sneaking-out sort of person back then. Plus, Eli's mom was nice. She made us chocolate chip cookies. They came from a log of premade dough, but still.

The other guys laughed. I didn't, and neither did Roby. I'd heard about kids who did crazy stuff like sneaking out and smoking weed and using acid – back then, that's how I would have said it – but I didn't want to do that shit. Back then, the thought of it made me break out in a cold sweat.

I remember how Roby's eyes met mine, and how that made me feel better.

At a quarter past ten, Eli tossed his game controller on the coffee table. Chaz, Trey, Joseph, and Monty – oh, yeah, Monty was there, too – did the same. So did I. So did Roby.

Eli opened the basement window and popped out the screen. He gave us eyeball directions, and one by one we leveraged ourselves up and out of the window. The ground was damp and left wet circles on the knees of my pants.

Eli stayed in the shadows and scuttled to the dark asphalt of his cul-de-sac. When the rest of us caught up, he grinned. His teeth were too small, as small as baby teeth.

"There's a convenience store that's open till midnight, but we can't go in all at the same time," he instructed us in a bossy voice. "We'll go in two by two. Get whatever you can. Just shove it in your pockets. Then we'll go to the liquor store and see if we can persuade someone to buy us beer."

"If we find a homeless dude, we can bribe him with the food we steal," said Chaz.

"Exactly," said Eli.

He cut across a neighbor's yard. The others trailed behind him. My feet slowed of their own accord, and

Roby hung back with me. That was the beautiful thing. That's what made everything all right.

We stopped where we were and let the others go on without us. I texted Mom, and she picked me and Roby up, no questions asked. At school on Monday, Eli and Chaz called us pussies, but Monty found us in the cafeteria and told us nothing had happened. He and the others had hung around the parking lot of the convenience store, Monty said, until finally Eli went in and bought a Mars bar.

No homeless man was bribed.

No beer was obtained.

"*Tchh,*" Monty said in that dismissive way that only certain guys can pull off. "You guys missed *nada,* believe me."

If Roby were here, we could laugh about that night. After that, we could laugh about me and the mess I've made of my life. Although if Roby were here, would I be in this mess? I wouldn't, there's no way I would, and that said so much about Roby – and so much about me.

Christmas came and went in a haze of Kpins, alcohol, and even a little oxy. Then it was January, and I thought, *New year, new beginning.* I told myself that this time I could do it. I could have a fresh start. My eighteenth birthday was four months out, and I swore to myself that this time I was going to quit for real. Then, knowing I was going to quit, I gave myself permission for one last binge.

After taking all the Klonopin I had in my possession and topping it off with a warm beer I found in my closet, I went upstairs to ask Mom for some Ambien. I knocked on the door to her bedroom. She cracked it open, already in her pajamas.

"Did I wake you?" I asked.

"No," she said. "Why?"

"Just, I was wondering..." I sighed. "I'm having a hard time falling asleep."

"Oh, sweetheart," Mom said. She thought I couldn't sleep because of Roby, that I was still recovering from Roby's death. That was true. I'd always be recovering from Roby's death. So every so often, she gave me a single Ambien and made me promise to take it and get straight into bed.

Tonight she frowned, and then did exactly that. I knew she felt like she was a bad mom for giving me drugs, and I felt like shit for playing her. I told myself that this was the last time.

She ducked away, then returned and handed me a

small oval pill, saying, "You have to go straight to bed after you take it, because it has a rapid onset. I mean it, Paul. You have to climb under the covers and turn off the lights immediately."

"Ma, of course," I said. She worried that if I didn't, I'd go into an Ambien-induced fugue state and eat raw chicken straight from the refrigerator, like some lady she saw on *Oprah*. I knew better. Ambien makes you trip if you stay awake, but tripping doesn't make you eat raw chicken. If you eat it anyway, that's on you.

"Of course what?" Mom prompted, and I pushed my knuckles against my forehead. I had to repeat her instructions back to her? For real?

"Of course I'll go straight to bed. That's why I need it, so I can..."

The floor rippled beneath me.

"Paul?"

"So ... so I can..."

The house turned sideways, and the floor rose up and slammed my face. I heard Mom gasp. I saw the fibers of the carpet, a sea of beige tendrils.

"Paul? Paul!"

I didn't pass out, but only just barely. My head was made of sand.

Mom dragged me to a sitting position. She propped me against the wall. I tried to balance my head on the head stalk of my neck, but it kept lolling to the side.

Mom held a glass of water to my lips. I drank.

"Paul, I love you," she said. Her eyes swam with tears. "Will you please, please tell me what's going on?"

I started to say I was dehydrated, I was overtired, I'd stayed up too late working on homework. *I'm exhausted, that's all, I swear.* But the worry in her face undid me.

"Mama," I said. "I need your help."

chapter thirty-seven

We're in this together," Mom insisted during the baddest of the bad.

Were we, though? I mean, I'm glad she didn't kick me out of the house. I'm glad she didn't tell Dad, though she told me she would, 100 percent, if I didn't get clean.

But Mom wasn't the one whose life was falling apart. I was.

"I found you a therapist," she told me not long after the Ambien night. "His name's Todd, and he's really down-to-earth."

"No," I said.

"He understands kids, because he has kids of his own. One of his sons even spent time in jail, he told me."

"That's a great endorsement. He can't help his own kids, but somehow he's going to help me?"

"Paul, talking to people helps."

"Mom, that's not going to happen. I'm not going to talk to some grown-up who's going to judge me and tell me what a shitty person I am." I already knew what a shitty person I was. No way could I sit in some office and have every single layer of shit ripped off.

"Todd's not like that. He's —"

"I said no! God! Can you hear me?"

I stormed downstairs, because I hated the way she looked at me these days. Her eyes, her anxious, fearful eyes. The way she'd start to speak, then break off, as if she was afraid I would bite her head off if she said the wrong thing. Oh, and she always and only said the wrong things.

She pitched her next idea a few days later. "I've done some more research," she said, probing my expression. "How much clonazepam have you been taking?"

I scowled and turned away. I reached into the pantry and grabbed a box of Fruity Pebbles, only someone –

me – had left both the box and the inner lining open, so the Fruity Pebbles were stale.

I crammed a handful in my mouth and spoke around them. "Six milligrams."

"Six milligrams a day?" Mom said. Too late, she tried to mask her dismay.

"Yes, Mom, a day. And yes, Mom, it's bad. Like I said."

"Well, you can't stop taking them all at once," she said.

I tried to lift my eyebrows. My eyelids were too heavy. I couldn't. "You think I don't know that? Mom, I'm not an idiot."

She started to say something, then thought better of it. I could tell she was trying to remain calm, but her slow breathing techniques made ants crawl over my skin. I scratched my scalp, digging my fingers in deep.

"All right, well, there's a prescription drug that can help with benzodiazepine dependence," Mom said. "It's called Flumazenil. We can talk to Dr. McKurdy, and he can wean you down from your six-milligram dose."

"All right, well, that's never going to happen," I said, mimicking her stupid tone. I crumbled the cereal liner and crammed it down hard. "I know about Flumazenil.

I've done all the same research you have. But no way in hell am I going to Dr. McKurdy."

"Paul," Mom chided.

"No way. Never." Dr. McKurdy has been my doctor for as long as I can remember, and he is without a doubt the nicest doctor on the planet. He used liquid nitrogen to freeze a wart on my finger when I was little. I thought it was the coolest thing.

Mom blinked rapidly. "Then what do you propose?"

"That we both accept that I'm fucked," I said angrily. "You're not helping, Mom. At all."

Mom bowed her head. Several seconds ticked by. "We will figure this out," she said in a tight voice. "Can we please be kind to each other while we do?"

I pushed the box of Fruity Pebbles with the tip of my index finger, and it toppled over.

"Yeah. Sure. Whatever," I said. "But right now I'm going to take a nap." I strode toward the basement stairs. I stopped and turned around. "Oh, and Mom?"

"Yes?" The way she looked at me, the glimmer of hope... *oh shit.* She thought I was going to apologize or try to make peace. My head buzzed in the new way it did, like bees were inside me. "Eight milligrams."

"I'm sorry?" she said.

"Eight milligrams a day, that's how much I've been taking. Not six." I stood there, staring at her as she stared at me. I clenched my fists and left the kitchen.

Every night, she tiptoed into my bedroom and put her hand on my forehead. If I wasn't asleep, I pretended I was so she couldn't talk to me. I knew she wanted to know where I was getting the benzos, since she had to know I was still taking them, but she didn't ask. So, maybe I was wrong and she didn't want to know. Maybe I'd lost the status of being her sweet boy, and she didn't want to know that I was selling my swag for drugs.

A week and a half later, on a Saturday, she made me go with her to Straus Lake, where as a kid I'd spent long days swimming and fooling around. There was a shallow side and a deep side of the lake, the two halves separated by a long wooden pier. To earn the privilege of swimming on the deep side, you had to swim to shore from the end of the pier while a lifeguard walked alongside you, keeping an eye on you from above.

When I first took the test, I choked. Not literally. Not on lake water. Just, as soon as I'd slid into the lake from the far end of the pier, the sandy shore seemed impossibly distant. In reality, it was a fourth of a mile away. Swimming a fourth of a mile in a single uninterrupted stretch wasn't easy, not when you couldn't put your feet down if you needed a break, or if you simply wanted a break. It was doable, though. I'd done it multiple times on the shallow side of the lake.

On the day I took the test, there wasn't a cloud in the sky. The sun glinted off the water in bright white bursts, blinding me when I craned my neck to make sure the lifeguard was where she was supposed to be. Her name was Suzette, and while the other lifeguards were friendly and liked to laugh, Suzette was always grumpy. She never gave warnings to kids who splashed too much or dunked each other. She just blew her whistle and ordered the offenders out. She was the one lifeguard I'd hoped wouldn't administer my swim test, but too bad, so sad. She was the lifeguard I got.

"Mom," I'd pleaded, tugging on her arm. I was seven. In the fall, I'd start second grade.

Mom, who wasn't a fan of Suzette either, had smiled encouragingly. "You've got this, Paul-o," she said.

I couldn't spot Suzette when I searched for her from the water, and I couldn't make out the shore ahead of me, although I knew it was there. My panic ramped up, and it grew hard to get a full breath of air. Finally I caved, treading water and fumbling for Suzette's lifeguard pole, which she jabbed toward me with disdain.

"You have to return to the shallow end," she decreed. "You can retest, but not today."

I clutched the pole like a soggy koala bear, twining my arms and legs around it.

"You're close enough to stand, you know," Suzette said.

I blinked and got my bearings. The shore was five feet away.

I let go of the pole, and my feet found the silty, squelchy lake bottom. I trudged out of the water to where Mom waited with open arms.

"Now you know that tomorrow, when you take the test for real, you'll ace it," she said, as if swimming alongside Suzette had been nothing but a practice run. She hugged me. "Well done, buddy."

That day I'd plowed out of the lake feeling small and stupid. Then Mom worked her Mom Magic and made everything better. Today I towered over her, but on the inside, where it counted, I was a baby.

It was the end of January, and the weather was brisk. We were the only ones there. We sat on a wooden swing, which Mom tried to get going, but I planted my feet on the ground and bent forward, my elbows on my knees and my chin in my hands.

Mom sighed. She held a purse in her lap, which was weird. Mainly she shoved her phone and debit card into the back pocket of her jeans and was good to go.

She unfastened the purse clasp, and it opened like a mouth. She pulled out a small package wrapped in brown paper.

"Mom?" I said.

She pulled away the paper to reveal a bunch of blister packs of small blue pills, held together with a rubber band. The words on the foil backing were foreign. Not French foreign or Spanish foreign, but foreign-with-a-whole-new-alphabet foreign.

I looked at Mom, and my heart skipped a beat. This was my mother. My mom. With pills she hadn't bought through legal means, I was pretty sure. Actually, I was positive.

"We'll wean you off the Klonopin together," she said, each word a stone.

"Mom, I can't believe you bought illegal drugs."

For half a second, fury warped her features. "Well, I did. What else was I supposed to do?"

My heart raced. Sweat broke out everywhere.

I shrunk back, but Mom grabbed me. She dug her fingernails into my arm.

"Mom," I managed. "You're scaring me."

"You're. My. Son," she said. She let me go, flinging my arm away from her.

Tears rushed to my eyes. A terror filled my chest like never before. Where was my mom? What had I done to my mom?

"I'll be your health provider or counselor or whatever you want to call it," she said.

"Okay," I said. "Yes."

In the cool, clear air, we sat together on the swing and she told me the rules. We would follow the protocol outlined in a detox program she'd found online. She'd dole out the appropriate amount of Valium – that's what the pills were – for week one, week two, and so on. Valium, like Klonopin, is a benzo, but it has a longer half-life, which makes it easier when tapering down. It would stay in my bloodstream longer, Mom explained, so hopefully my withdrawal symptoms would be less severe.

"Also, Valium is the only drug I could get my hands on," Mom said. Her eyes narrowed. "So there you go."

"Momma..."

"No," Mom said. "We're doing this, end of story. Your job, Paul, is to be compliant. No more street drugs. No falling off the wagon. Can you promise me that?"

"I absolutely promise," I said in a wobbly voice. "I want this, too."

"From what I've read, it's not going to be fun. But you'll get through it." She loosened the rubber band around the stack of blister packs and pulled one pack free. It consisted of two rows of ten pills. She reached into her purse, pulled out a pair of safety scissors, and snipped at the pack in order to separate eight pills from one of the ten-pill rows. She handed the eight-pill portion to me.

"Each of these pills is ten milligrams of Valium," she said. "Ten milligrams of Valium are roughly equivalent to one milligram of Klonopin, so eight of these"–she tapped the pills–"should feel to your body like eight milligrams of Klonopin."

We gazed at the small blue pills.

"Jesus, Paul," Mom said. "That's a lot of pills."

My throat thickened. "Yeah."

She told me more stuff I already knew, about Valium versus Klonopin and sticking to a tapering schedule and how over time she would reduce the amount she gave me, until at last my body would be free and clear. She told me what to expect from withdrawal, which I also already knew. Night sweats, tremors, acute anxiety. Insomnia. Mood swings.

Hell, I deserved it.

"I guess that's it," Mom said half an hour later. She snapped her purse shut. "Any questions?"

"No questions."

"And you're in for the long haul?"

I dipped my head down, then up. "Yes." She seemed to want more, so I said, "I'm in for the long haul."

"You can't slip up. You have to take this seriously."

"I will. I am."

Mom's eyes welled. "Life is impossibly precious. You are impossibly precious." She took my hands. "Stay in this life as long as you can, Paul. Do you promise?"

"Mom," I said. My voice came out husky.

"Do you promise?" she repeated.

"Yes, Mom, I promise. You don't have to worry."

chapter
thirty-eight

I was on week one of my tapering schedule, with eleven weeks to go, and I hadn't experienced any crappy effects, which was a relief. But still, I was going through withdrawal. That's who I was now. That was my identity. I was seventeen years old, and like a complete dumbshit I'd gotten hooked on Kpin, and now I was basically in rehab, with my mother as the lead nurse-doctor person.

She doled out each day's supply of Valium with a stranger's eyes and so many held-back questions. Was I staying on the straight and narrow? Was I lying to her about how I was feeling? Was I going to make it through this alive, or was I going to slip forever into the seedy underbelly of dirty needles and toothless vagrants?

I mean, I got where she was coming from, but I could have done without the melodrama. I wanted to make this work as much as she did. I was going to make it work.

On week two of tapering down, I went stir-crazy. At first I thought it was just me. I didn't connect it to withdrawal. It became really hard to sit still in class, plus everything my teachers said was boring and useless as hell.

"Paul, please talk to me," Natalia said, catching me after my catering class one day. "Kahlia thinks there's something going on with you, and so do I."

"You and Kahlia and Gertrude and everyone else," I muttered.

"Yeah, because we care," Natalia said.

Fuck off, I thought. I couldn't stand her frightened I'm-a-saint-and-you're-a-degenerate act. If by accident we did make eye contact, her gaze seared me, I'm not even kidding. Like, inside my brain. My heart.

Gertrude, at least, looked at me like I was just a pathetic loser, which of course I was. I was a fucking disappointment to everyone.

"Natalia, chill," I said, clipping my words short. "I've got everything under control."

"Do you?" she pressed. Her hand hovered near my arm. "Because you don't seem like you do."

"But you aren't me, and I'd appreciate it if you'd quit roasting me." I scratched the back of my neck. "And Kahlia should mind her own business."

She withdrew her hand. "I'm worried about you. You need help."

I narrowed the distance between us and lowered my voice. "I'm getting help. I told my mom, all right? Are you happy?"

She'd flinched when I stepped closer, because she was scared of me. Or of me who wasn't me, but nonetheless was. It killed me. "That's great," she said. "I'm glad. Thank you."

I shook my head and strode off. I wasn't doing it for her. I slammed a locker with the side of my fist.

Four weeks into the weaning process, I realized what an idiot I'd been. Until that point, I'd been thinking, *Oh, this isn't so bad.*

But four weeks in, my body fell apart. All I thought about, all I was able to think about, was each new slice of misery as it came my way. I lived in bursts and pops of teeth-gritting pain or, conversely, in elasticized moments of time where each second became a mountainous drop of water clinging to the faucet of the sink, wobbling, swelling, before torturously breaking free and bursting on the basin below.

Sometimes I felt anxious to the nth degree. Anxious for no reason I could pin down, and yet my heart raced and I broke out in a sweat and I felt, literally, as if I might up and die.

"What is it, baby?" Mom said when she caught me pacing the house. I was trying to wear my panic out. Tire myself to the point that the panicky feelings would be extinguished. "I know you said you felt anxious, but anxious about what?"

I shook my head. "It's just … it's just an impending sense of doom, all right?"

"That sounds awful," Mom said. She gave me one of her don't-set-off-the-teenager looks. "And vague. Can you be more clear?"

"Mom, no," I snapped. "And, as I've told you five thousand times, your questions don't help."

She held her hands up and backed away, eyeing me with so much fucking concern.

I couldn't eat. When I did, I became a shitting

monster. So. Much. Shit. My asshole felt like it was on fire, and I knew – I knew – that if I just returned to my former daily dose of benzos, a sense of calm would wash everything away, even the shits. It sucked, knowing the way out and at the same time knowing that the way out would ultimately lead me right back into the hell I was trying to claw my way out of.

If the days were bad – and they were – the nights were unbearable. I started dreading going to bed even though I was bone-achingly tired, because my body refused to sleep. One minute I'd be shivering and pulling my sheet, blanket, and comforter over me like a cocoon. The next minute, I'd kick the covers off furiously, so hot I wanted to jump out of my skin.

When I slept, if I slept, I woke up to sweat-soaked sheets, sour and clammy. Every night I hauled myself out of bed and trudged to the bathroom to take a piss. When I went back to my room, I eyed my bed with hatred. Fucking bed. How the fuck could anyone sleep in cold, clammy sheets?

My muscles twitched randomly and violently. It probably looked as if I were having convulsions. I'd be sitting at my desk, trying so hard to think about anything other than how swollen my head felt or the weird burning sensation spreading over my entire body, and *bang*. My knee would jump and hit the bottom of my desk. Or my foot would spaz out, or a muscle I didn't know I had on my thigh would bulge and recede, bulge and recede, like a sick, blind creature trying to burst from my skin.

My joints ached. I had a headache to end all headaches, so much so that drilling a hole into my skull sounded like a good idea. I probably would have, if I owned a skull-drill and knew how to use it. Instead, I popped four Advil every four hours. It didn't make a dent.

Nothing. Made. A. Dent.

And. Oh, yeah. Possibly the most insane-making withdrawal symptom of all? "Restless leg syndrome." Such a misleadingly peppy name for a condition so hellish. I'd heard of restless leg syndrome before, but I never gave it any thought beyond, *Well, that sounds strange and annoying.*

It was so much more than strange and annoying.

This is what would happen: I'd reluctantly go to bed. Like I said, I started dreading the whole prospect of attempting to sleep early on in the weaning-off process, but I still had to try. There were too many empty hours to fill otherwise. Plus, I was exhausted. I felt like I had the flu all the time. But the flu feeling, I got somewhat used to. I've had the flu before. You bow your head and plow forward.

So I'd be in bed. I'd start off by lying on my back. Then an urge to shift positions would swell over me, only it wasn't an urge. It was an imperative. I couldn't NOT roll to my side.

Once on my side, I'd grit my teeth and screw shut my eyes, willing sleep to come and just fucking take me, only no. That awful wave would build inside me again, and I'd flip to my other side. Back and forth, back and forth, like a trout flailing on dry land.

On the worst nights, I'd shift positions relentlessly, and then – my legs. Oh my god, my legs. It wasn't restlessness. You can tamp down restlessness, like if you're feeling antsy and jittery in class, but you make yourself stop bouncing your leg or drumming your fingers.

I'd lie there, clenching my jaw and hating life and hating myself, and a dreadful urgency would mount, as if raw energy were trapped in my leg muscles, building and building, until there was nothing I could do but get up and march around my room like a fucking toy soldier. If I didn't, my legs would burst like balloons filled with too much helium.

The same thing sometimes happened with my arms, my biceps, and I'd have to slide to the floor and pump out a hundred push-ups in an attempt to extinguish the neural impulses firing throughout my muscle fibers. Restless legs, restless arms, restless everything. Restless Paul. Miserable Paul. Pathetic, idiotic, brought-it-on-myself Paul.

I hated this "me" who was Paul. Who wouldn't?

So many things sucked that first month and into the second. All of it sucked. I felt like shit. I missed Natalia. But what sucked the most was Roby's absence. It was so goddamn selfish of me, I know, but I missed the person I used to be when he was with me. He made me bigger, and also better.

I made him better and bigger, too, though.

I missed the "Paul" Roby saw in me. But just as much, I missed the person I'd felt myself become when I'd seen Roby as *Roby*. I missed being the person who saw Roby's best self.

Roby wouldn't have let me get into this mess.

Roby, I had a feeling, was the only person who could get me out of it. Only, Roby wasn't here.

chapter
thirty-nine

I started hanging out with this girl Cate, a fellow senior. Cate was tall and gaunt, with wide hips and a flat chest. Rumor had it she was a violin genius, or maybe cello. I wasn't sure, and I didn't bother to find out. I hung out with Cate because Cate knew what I was going through, because she was going through it, too.

Cate began with a bona fide prescription for Ativan, for stage fright. She told me she liked how the Ativan smoothed out her edges, so she started taking it for other reasons. Exam stress, anxiety at parties, you name it. Since her legitimate stash was limited, she cast her net wider, copping any type of benzodiazepine she caught a whiff of.

And so on and so on. At least half the kids in my senior class have dropped a xanny or Kpin at some point in their lives. I don't think adults fully appreciate that.

Cate was constantly strung out, both full of herself and needy as fuck at the same time. She was a lot, and it would be an overstatement to say I liked her.

But she'd decided to wean herself off benzos, too. She was decreasing her daily dose, same as me, but with a slightly more flexible tapering schedule and no adult involvement. She knew about brain zaps. She understood what I meant when I told her I had ants in my head, or beetles waving their long spindly legs around. The chills, the hot flashes, all of it. She felt as shitty as I did, and sometimes she even made jokes about it, like the day I arrived at school without my sense of balance. Other kids pulled away from me, as if my seasick stumbling was contagious. Cate laughed and called me a pirate.

Cate wasn't pretty, but she wasn't un-pretty, and so, yeah, we numbed ourselves with sex.

It wasn't good sex. It was skin against skin, parts against parts. But whatever.

Natalia reproached me with her large, liquid eyes.

Really, Paul? said her gaze when she saw Cate rest her head on my shoulder. *You and Benzo Bait Cate?*

Except Natalia probably didn't call Cate that, even in private.

Cate had lanky hair, and she introduced me to her other friends who had lanky hair. Not washing was a thing with Cate's crowd. Cate liked my hair, which was clean. I did manage to keep up with my basic hygiene, thank you very much. One night Cate invited me to a guy's house party, and I went. Why not?

We sat on a blue sofa. She ran her fingers through my hair.

"That feels good," I told her.

She skimmed her fingernails over my scalp, the way Natalia used to.

"That feels really good," I said. "Please don't stop. Nothing feels good anymore, ever. But what you're doing..."

"It helps?" Cate said.

I nodded heavily. "It helps."

She laughed. "We broke ourselves, didn't we? We are fucked."

"It'll get better, though," I said. I looked at her. "Won't it?"

"In a year, maybe. Maybe longer." She shrugged. "I've done the reading. Some people experience withdrawal symptoms for the rest of their lives."

My vision tunneled, spirals inside spirals inside spirals. I could not. I absolutely could not live like this until the end of my days. "Fu-u-u-uck," I said.

"You know, though," she said.

I squinted. It was something in her tone. "What?"

"What are you down to, dosage wise?"

"Two ten-mil Valiums a day." I thrust my fist into the air. "Woot. Rockstar."

"Nice," Cate said.

Around us, people danced. Music blared. Cate moved her hand from my head to my neck. She massaged my tight muscles.

"That means you've gotten rid of your tolerance," she said casually. "You could take half a xan, a fourth of a xan, and have all your symptoms go away"–she snapped–"like that, just for tonight."

She peered at me. My pulse quickened.

"I'm the same," she said. "And what the hell? I've gotten this far, I deserve a reward."

"Cate—"

"I'm not saying you have to. Ha. No, dude, what you do

is on you. Just..." She dug into her pocket and pulled out a round white pill. "Wanna split it? I've only got this one, so even if we wanted to get hooked again, we couldn't."

It was a pill. Just a pill, and I couldn't tear my eyes from it. Half a xan and I could sleep tonight. Half a xan and my brain would shut up for a hot minute. Half a xan would give me a temporary break, and I'd come back stronger. And, like Cate said, we couldn't fall back on that train even if we wanted to.

I snapped the pill in two and crunched my half like candy. I didn't regret it. I rejoiced in it. Within thirty minutes, I felt better, and the relief was so monumental, so huge...

"Oh my god," I groaned, my head sinking into the sofa cushion.

I called Mom and told her I was spending the night at Monty's house.

"Paul, I'm so glad you're reconnecting with him," Mom said. "Friends are important. All of us need friends." Her tone turned uncertain. "But you're sure...? You will make good decisions, right?"

"Mom. Of course."

"You can't mask what you're going through with other drugs," she said. "No alcohol, no weed, no anything."

"Mo-o-o-om," I said. Cate popped open a Miller Lite and handed it to me.

"Well, have fun," she said. It cost her something. I won't pretend I didn't know. "I love you, baby. And I trust you."

"As you should." My head felt unclogged for the first time in weeks. "I'll see you tomorrow, Mama. Your boy's got this under control."

chapter
forty

That spring, when by Mom's calculations I was finally benzo-free, she surprised me by announcing a celebratory trip to Atlanta.

"I'm just so proud of you," she said. "We'll stay with Grandmommy and Granddaddy. We'll go shopping at Lenox Square. We both know Lenox has better stores than Brevard."

She beamed, mistaking my expression for dazed delight. "We'll take a break from normal life. We deserve to! We'll leave this Friday and stay through the weekend. Sound good, Paul-o?"

My first thought was, *Oh, shit. There is no way.*

Like a little kid skipping down a sidewalk littered with shards of glass, I'd stepped straight back into benzo dependence. My fall was as predictable as fuck, with Natalia shaking her head from the sidelines. Unlike Mom, who I guess was happy in her "yay, recovery!" bubble, Natalia knew what the score was.

But lying to Mom was one thing. Lying to Grandmom and Granddad ... the thought made my soul lurch. Being at my grandparents' house meant running around in footie pajamas, the smell of brownies, the steady tick of the grandfather clock. The wrought-iron balustrade that led upstairs, my palm skimming the gleaming cherry handrail. A guest room just for me. Sheets printed with sailboats. Little soaps shaped like bird eggs, nestled in a nest of twigs.

I couldn't go back there, not from where I stood now. Grandmom and Granddad have only ever seen the Good Me. Being faded in their presence broke the laws of the universe.

I called Cate. She told me I was tripping and to chill out. I tried to explain, my words skittering over each other, until Cate cut me off, saying, "Honestly, Paul? I couldn't care less about your precious relationship with your precious grandparents. If you're stressing about the xans, then don't take them anymore."

"Go cold turkey?" I said.

"If you don't want drugs in your system, then yeah," retorted Cate. "I'm hanging up now. Bye."

I considered my predicament. With Mom as my recovery cheerleader, I'd gotten down to twenty milligrams of Valium a day, which was equivalent to two milligrams of Klonopin, which was a big accomplishment.

These days my intake varied, but I was easily back up to four milligrams a day and often more.

I was fucked, again.

I hated myself, again.

But it was what it was. I learned about the Atlanta trip on Monday. On Tuesday, I took two Kpins instead of three. On Wednesday, I limited myself to one, and on Thursday, using immense willpower, I popped half a xanny, meaning a measly one milligram of Xanax went into my system. Basically I did a rapid taper. It wasn't ideal, but what part of this was?

At school on Friday, I felt pumped despite the queasiness my nervous system was throwing at me. There was residual medication in my body, but it would be gone soon enough. Then I'd be drug-free. If I didn't take more drugs from this point onward, I'd stay drug-free. This was an accomplishment worth celebrating. Mom was right. Atlanta! Yeah! Woof!

At home, I threw a weekend's worth of clothes into my backpack, including a pair of nice pants and a dress shirt since Granddad would surely take us someplace fancy for dinner on one of the nights. A wave of dizziness hit me hard, and I dropped to a crouch, knees bent and fingers on the floor for balance. I opened my eyes when the dizziness left and saw that the fibers of the carpet were breathing. Uh-oh.

The effect passed, and I made a mental note to chug a glass of orange juice before we headed out. Back when I was in the thick of it, I'd had some strange vision tics. Sometimes a slice of someone's face was blanked out, other times my vision doubled. I didn't know for sure that those symptoms were related to low blood sugar, but as I hadn't eaten all day, I figured there might be a connection.

When we left Brevard and started down the mountain road that would take us to the interstate, my chest inflated and I felt a surge of optimism. Regal pine trees formed a canopy above us, with only patches of blue sky breaking through. As was often the case on this stretch of the drive, ours was the only car on the road. I felt free. I was leaving my crap life behind me, and ahead of me was a clean slate.

I tapped out the beat of the Mumford & Sons song Mom was playing. She'd gotten a system update, or maybe a new streaming app, and it was awesome. Actual musical notes – well, no, probably holographs – floated from the speakers, then broke apart and dispersed when they hit the roof. Emojis, too. A winky face breezed past me. Then a yellow smiley face. I smiled back.

"Mom," I said. I laughed, and my own laugh burbled up and shaped itself into line drawings of triangles and squares. "Seriously the coolest app ever."

"What app, honey?" Mom asked.

I drummed my fingers against the armrest. I pushed out the beat with my toes, inside my sneakers. The song pulsed through me. Shapes and emojis drifted like dandelion fluff through the air, and then actual dandelion fluff floated through the air. Well, no, probably holographs of dandelion fluff.

"Amazing," I said.

"I agree," Mom said, glancing at me with a smile. "I love this song."

At the halfway point between Brevard and Atlanta,

we stopped for snacks at the Food Lion, its aisles lit with bright white fluorescent lighting. Mom went one way, looking for coffee drinks, and I went in search of chips, ideally Pringles, which were both delicious and fun. If you put two Pringles in your mouth at opposite angles, you could make a duck mouth. *Quack.*

A woman wearing hipster bell bottoms and a plaid shirt approached me, her cart overflowing with cereal boxes. She looked familiar, but I couldn't work out how I knew her.

"Paul," she said. "So nice to see you!"

It was Ms. Summers, my ninth-grade WEB teacher. "Ms. Summers! Wow!" I said. "What's up?"

"Would you like to buy some weed?" she asked, gesturing at her cart. The cereal boxes were just for show, forming Cap'n Crunch walls around a dozen or so plastic planters sprouting pot. It was a clever trick. I was impressed. But I had the idea that I shouldn't buy pot from a teacher, even if we weren't on school grounds. Also, what if Mom saw?

My heart hammered against my rib cage, and I spun on my heel. When I found Mom at the cash register, my skin was dimpling from cold sweat. I rubbed the back of my hand across my forehead.

"Paul?" Mom said. Her hair was too bright. The ends fluttered with static electricity. She said more stuff, but I couldn't keep up, and I wondered briefly if I should come clean, confess that her boy was feeling all kinds of floaty.

No. I felt paranoid from seeing Ms. Summers, that's all. Maybe I should have bought just a little weed from her?

Mom's hand on my shoulder. Heavy. I looked at it and knew it and said, "I'm fine. I'm good. Just hungry."

That was the right answer, because her face stretched into a happy Silly Putty shape.

"Let's get some food in you," she said.

In the car, I shoveled chips into my mouth. When my fingers collected little dots of salt and crunchy potato bits, I twisted sideways and dusted off my hands. That way, Mom's bunny could eat the crumbs. I hadn't realized Mom had brought a bunny, but I guess that was up to her. Anyway it was a cute bunny, with long floppy ears and a twitching nose.

Ohhh. It was Lily's bunny. Lily from school. Lily had given the bunny to Ms. Summers, and Ms. Summers had given the bunny to us. Right. Was I in charge of taking care of it, or was Mom? I had the sense I shouldn't ask, because asking would get Ms. Summers in trouble. Because of the weed.

I sat back in my seat, facing forward. We were on a flat highway now. Twilight roared past. Trees loomed and turned violent. I screwed shut my eyes.

"Paul?" Mom said.

"I really did see Ms. Summers," I said. I needed her to understand that. I wasn't acting crazy, it was just – the bunny. I was worried about the bunny.

"When?" Mom said.

"Huh?"

"Ms. Summers, your teacher? Paul, I'm confused."

"Yeah-yeah, my bad." I fluttered my fingers, and each finger cast behind it a trail of glitter lights. Was I tripping? Had I dropped a tab of acid and forgotten?

Other cars now shared the highway. I saw the first green-and-white sign for Atlanta, fourteen miles away. When we crossed into city limits, the highway would gain lanes and the cars would multiply, all of them streaking past.

Pull it together, buddy.

Paul, I'm confused.

I must have dozed off, only my dreams draped

themselves over reality, giving everything a sodden, unreal texture. When I woke, it was with a start.

"Mom! The bunny!" I exclaimed.

"What?" Mom said. "What bunny?"

I checked the back seat. No bunny, no bunny. My breaths came erratically. "Lily's bunny, I promised her I'd take care of it!"

"Who's Lily?" Mom asked. "Do I know Lily?"

"Yes, Mom." Impatience fought at me like gnats. "Lily has a bunny, and she cuddles it, and Roby said ..." I felt a flash of terror as the pieces came together. "Roby! We left Roby behind!"

I twisted violently, searching for him out my window. Roby had Lily's bunny – of course, Roby had Lily's bunny! Roby was in charge of Lily's bunny, just as I was in charge of him, only I'd screwed up royally and left him behind. I could see him, just barely, small and distant on the side of the road.

I pounded the window. "Mom, turn around!"

At the sight of her baffled expression, I pushed air from my lungs in a howl and scrabbled to open my door.

"Paul!" Mom screamed.

Air rushed past as the highway unspooled beneath me. Mom swerved, throwing me back against my seat and then forward against my seat belt. She leaned over me, her shoulder pressing against my Adam's apple. Her face was white. I couldn't breathe.

She pulled my door closed. The car veered from side to side.

Horns blared, brakes whined, and colors far too vibrant kaleidoscoped around me. Mom gripped the wheel and gobbled asphalt. Gravel crunched when we hit the emergency lane, white hot kernels of popcorn jumping everywhere as the car screeched to a stop.

Too late, too late, sang the sudden silence.

I crumpled forward over the dashboard and sobbed.

chapter
forty-one

S o, Paul," Dr. Mackey said, his blue eyes locked on mine. "How are you today? Are you feeling more like yourself?"

I had on an old pair of sweats Mom had dug up and a soft white T-shirt that belonged to Granddad. An undershirt, technically. Granddad wore them beneath his button-downs. I was probably well enough to talk to Dr. Mackey downstairs, not up here in the guest room that had been mine since I was a little boy, but I wasn't ready to leave the safety of bed.

I ran my thumb over the hem of my sheet. When Grandmommy puts sheets on beds, she does it the way where the patterned side of the fitted sheet faces up and the patterned side of the top sheet faces down. I was cocooned between ocean waves and cheerful sailboats. I felt safe, relatively speaking.

I also felt tremendously ashamed.

However, as best as I could tell, I was no longer hallucinating. "My mind feels ... spongy," I said. "Like, dull. Not that I'm the sharpest knife in the block on the best of days."

Dr. Mackey regarded me kindly. He was new to me, a friend of Granddad and Grandmom's who was a psychiatrist, and who was willing to make a house call for the sake of their fucked-up grandson. "That foggy feeling will get better. You'll have to begin fresh with the weaning process, which means going through withdrawal again, unfortunately. But you're young. You're resilient. You'll get through it."

I studied the decorative stitching on the comforter. The sailboats matched the sailboats on the sheets. I sighed.

"I've given your mom the name of a doctor in Brevard, a colleague of mine who will take over from here," Dr. Mackey said. "She's up to speed on the best practices for addiction recovery. You'll be in good hands."

"Okay," I said. I was still wrapping my head around

how public my fucked-up-ness had become. I had my flip-out moment in the car on Friday. Today was Sunday. Over the past two days, Mom had told my grandparents – who were her parents, she reminded me – the dirty truth about me. She'd caught Dad up, too. He and I spoke on the phone. It was awkward and awful. He was going to drive to Brevard next weekend. And I guess Mom and Dr. Mackey had put together a whole treatment plan for when we returned to North Carolina.

"Everything out in the open," Mom had informed me. "Everything aboveboard. You'll meet weekly with Dr. Webster, who will supervise your taper. If she thinks you need urine tests, then you'll have urine tests. I'll set you up with a therapist, and you *will* go talk to him. We can look into other support systems as needed."

She'd brushed my hair off my face. "We're doing it right this time."

"Mom..." I'd protested.

She told me that she was going to get counseling, too, to help her figure out how she factored into everything that had happened and to help her figure out "how to adopt positive strategies going forward." She told me that while she'd been horrified to bring her delusional son home to her parents, she also saw it as a gift, because it forced her to see what was going on with me.

I got the sense that Grandmom and Granddad had been firm with Mom about how she needed to be firm with me. Maybe one day I'll find humor in that, Mom's parents giving Mom parenting lessons even now. But mainly they'd given Mom support.

Along with shame, I felt a loosening within me. Maybe it was relief?

"Listen, Paul," Dr. Mackey said. "I'm going to call your mom and your grandparents in here in a second. They all want to check on you. But first I want to help you understand, from a medical perspective, what's going on with you. Okay?"

I lifted one shoulder.

"Imagine you're driving a car," Dr. Mackey said. "You're old enough to drive, right?"

Yes, I was old enough to drive. No, I wasn't, technically, driving yet. Whatever. No way was I getting into all of that.

"Yeah," I said.

"Imagine you've got your right foot pressed all the way down on the gas pedal, but at the same time, you're using your left foot to press as hard as you can on the brakes." He used his hands to demonstrate, angling both forward from his wrists. "The gas pedal, that's your body, doing its thing. But life throws a lot of stimuli at us, and I'm guessing that you're a sensitive guy, am I right?"

I lifted my eyebrows. I was listening.

"So you turned to benzodiazepines – Klonopin, Xanax, Ativan – to tamp down on all of that noise," said Dr. Mackey. He wiggled his left hand. "You put on the brakes, so to speak. When you stopped taking the pills —" He pantomimed something blowing up, complete with sound effects.

"All hell broke loose," he said. "Your body was still going full throttle, but you'd let up on the brakes entirely. There was residual medication in your system for a few days, but from what your mom's told me about your timeline, you couldn't have planned it better if you tried."

"Huh," I said. Mom had called Natalia, who called Cate, who actually got in touch with Mom, somewhat to my surprise. Cate was straight with Mom about my relapse, and Mom passed along the sordid details to Dr. Mackey and everyone else.

I swallowed. "I didn't plan it, believe me. None of this was intentional."

"No, I suppose not," Dr. Mackey said. He smiled. "No

one seeks out a psychotic break on purpose, do they?"

My stomach lurched. Psychotic break, for real?

"You saw things that weren't there," Dr. Mackey said. "A bunny, I think? In the back seat of your mom's car?"

My face grew hot.

"From what I understand, you experienced auditory hallucinations as well," Dr. Mackey continued. "Conversations that didn't really happen, sounds that only you heard?"

I knew Dr. Mackey wasn't intending to roast me, but I felt ripped open and laid bare.

I swallowed. "So ... you said my mom's out there? Waiting to see me?"

Dr. Mackey's gaze flicked to the hall, then landed back on me. "I imagine it was very scary," he said.

My throat thickened.

"I'll pass you over to your mom in a minute," Dr. Mackey said. "But, Paul, what I want you to know – none of this is your fault."

My breath made an ugly hitching sound, as I was pretty sure all of it was my fault.

"You didn't choose addiction," he said. "Nobody chooses addiction, and benzos, downers, they're a particularly nasty beast. Grabs hold and doesn't let go, hmm?"

I gave the smallest of nods.

"You made some bad choices. I won't argue with you there," he said. "But be kind to yourself, Paul. You've got a lot of life ahead of you, and it's your job to live it."

He left the room, and I heard him discussing something with Mom. I couldn't make out the words.

Granddad appeared in the doorway. After a slight hesitation, he approached the bed. The pressure in my chest was excruciating.

"David tells us you're feeling better?" he said in his normal no-nonsense voice. Only this wasn't normal. There was a sheet of glass between us. I was on one side. He was on the other.

I cleared my throat. "Not great, but yeah, definitely better."

"Glad to hear it," Granddad said. He reached through the glass and clapped his hand on my shoulder. "What do you say we make a run to Krispy Kreme, bring home some doughnuts, fresh off the grease? I think your mother and your grandmother could use the sugar."

Tears sprung to my eyes. *Oh*, I thought, as so many emotions, not all of them bad, juddered through me.

I swung my legs off the bed, leveraged my torso upright, and pressed my palms against the edge of the mattress. I pushed myself up.

chapter
forty-two

When I reached my one-month clean mark, Natalia met me for lunch at Rocky's Soda Shop. I ordered the Elvis, which is a grilled peanut-butter-and-banana sandwich, as well as a bacon cheeseburger and a chocolate malt.

Natalia ordered a vanilla milkshake.

As the waitress walked off, Natalia crinkled her nose. "Dang, Paul," she said. "Hungry much?"

I gave her the biggest smile. "I've missed the way you crinkle your nose."

"What?" She touched her nose. "I don't crinkle my nose."

"You do. It's adorable." My vision went blurry, but I pressed on. This was what life looked like now. Everything was raw and emotional, all the time. If I clammed up every time my throat got cloggy or my eyes got teary, I'd have to stop talking altogether and be a mime.

I would make a really bad mime.

"It's good to see you, Natalia," I said.

There must have been something in my expression that gave her pause, because she threw me a strange look. "That's the most honest I've heard you be since —" She flattened her hands on the laminate tabletop. "Since Roby died."

I nodded. It was as if, for nearly the entire last year, I'd been going around with mesh screens over my eyes, made from a material so thin and flexible that I hadn't realized they were there. The screens were gunky and smudged, which made the world look gunky and smudged.

When I came back to being me, the world came back too, sparkling and new.

I still wished Roby was in it. If I could bring back Roby, I'd bring him back so fucking hard.

A tear rolled down my cheek. Natalia was off her stool and at my side in a heartbeat. She wrapped her arms around me, and I rested my cheek in the nook between her chin and her chest. When we were dating, that was the way we often hugged, but in reverse. Natalia used to love to bury her head in the nook between my chin and my chest.

"Thanks," I said.

She drew back. She looked at me questioningly, letting one hand linger on my forearm.

"You have such pretty hands," I said. "They're so small."

She pulled away. She shrugged. "That's the way I was born."

"Yeah." I propped my elbow on the table and offered her my palm. "I'm glad you were born."

She knew me so well, even after I'd lost myself and almost wasn't found. She gazed at me, and I saw the ache in her just as she saw the ache in me.

She pressed her palm to mine.

"See?" I said. "Small."

"Or yours are just big."

"I guess both, huh?"

Our food arrived, and she withdrew her hand. I ate my cheeseburger. She sipped her milkshake.

"Do the thing with the cherry stem," I said.

"No thanks."

"Please?"

She cocked her head. "I don't want to, Paul. Really."

There was a time when I would have pushed her, would have goaded her by saying, "You can't do it anymore, can you? Barnard girls don't do party tricks, and Barnard girls sure as hell don't tie cherry stems into knots with their tongues."

I took another bite of my cheeseburger. I chewed, swallowed, and smiled at her. "Barnard, Natalia. You did it. That's awesome."

She looked pleased, but also uncomfortable. "What about you? What are you going to do?"

"Oh, you know. Eat. Drink. Live."

"You know what I mean."

I took a sip of her milkshake. "I think I'll get my driver's license. That's one thing."

Natalia gave a series of happy claps in that way that girls, but never boys, do. "Hey! Excellent!"

"And, you know, not be a fucking addict."

Her smile fell away.

"Hey, now," I warned. "Don't go knocking a man's goals."

She dropped her eyes. I waited until she looked at me again and said, "It's all good. I've been mowing the

Smalls' lawn and doing the yard work Roby used to do. When fall comes, there'll be more to do."

"That's really nice," Natalia said. "My mom has sent me over with food a couple of times. I think it's more so that they can see me than to give them meals." A shadow clouded her face. "Like, so there's still a teenager in their life, even if it's not the same."

Not the same. Never the same.

"Walking into their house, smelling their house – it's so weird," Natalia said.

"Because it smells like Roby?"

"Not just Roby, but yeah."

The first time I went to the Smalls' house after Roby died, I was scared shitless. I lifted my hand to the door, but I didn't knock.

The door opened anyway, and Roby's mom smiled painfully and invited me in. Everything hit me at once: the smells, the furniture, the framed photos of Roby from when he was a preemie all the way through junior year.

How do you get over that? How does anyone get over that?

You don't.

You keep going, but you never get over it.

"I'm going to start applying for jobs," I said. "When I save enough money, I'll buy a diamond watch or something. Boy's gotta have his swag."

She gazed at me from under her long lashes. "Once a swag boy, always a swag boy, huh?"

My cheeks grew warm. I still said stupid things. I probably always would.

Natalia looped a strand of hair around her finger. "I'm proud of you, Paul. I'm so glad you're here, so glad you're safe. And it's okay if you're not exactly happy, I think? Maybe you're on the way to being happy?"

"Yeah, for sure."

I understand that no one knows how much time they have on this earth. I understand that sometimes you have to act. But sometimes it's okay to be patient.

"Was it awful?" Natalia asked. "On the web, it said that getting off benzodiazepines is harder than getting off almost any other drug. Harder than heroin."

"It was bad. Still is, some days worse than others." I tugged my ear. "Some of the symptoms might not ever go away, my psychiatrist said."

"What? That's not fair."

I laughed wryly. "Yeah, well. I have tinnitus, for example. Tinnitus is —"

"I know what tinnitus is," Natalia said. "It's when your ears ring. It happens to old people."

"And people who screw up the neurons in their auditory cortex." I gestured at myself with my thumbs. "Who has tinnitus? This guy!"

"So you hear a ringing sound in your ears? All the time?"

"I use a white noise app when I go to bed. It helps a little." I took a big breath, then exhaled. "Um, I don't want in any way to hurt your feelings, but I'd rather not talk about this stuff, as it turns out."

I looked at her. *Okay?*

She nodded. *Okay.*

A moment passed. She said, "I saw your mom at Harris Teeter. She's really proud of you, too. She told me she wanted to do something to celebrate your one-month mark, like maybe go with you to get a tattoo?"

"I'm thinking about it," I said. A tattoo could be cool, if I figured out the right design with the right meaning. "But if I get one, I'll do it on my own. Can't be a mama's boy forever."

Natalia grinned. "Do you remember when your mom would drop you off at school – at *high school* – and she'd call out, 'Love you!' from the window of the car?"

I gazed at her, and my heart ached at all the things we knew about each other, all the memories that would be a part of us even if we drifted apart. Even *as* we drifted apart.

"You always said 'love you' back, even if you were ten feet away," Natalia said. "Even knowing that other kids could hear."

I thought about Mom, and now other emotions washed over me: shame, anger, grief. Gratitude.

I dipped my head. I smiled. "Yeah, well, she's my mom."

That night after dinner, I dug through my closet and pulled out my purple Bathing Ape bucket hat, the one I didn't wear to Roby's funeral.

It was crumpled. It was still pretty awesome.

In the backyard, I sat with my back against a tree and tugged my hat onto my head. A firefly blinked. Then another. The night drew darker. The stars came out. I imagined Roby, sitting beside me. Then I imagined Roby's body breaking into billions of atoms that rose in the sky.

I reached out to him. *Roby?* I searched and prodded,

and then, deciding it was the leap of faith that mattered, told him, *You're okay, buddy. I'm here.*

From inside the house, I heard Mom singing. Something small and warm opened in my chest, unfurling its petals like a flower that only blooms in moonlight.

I sat like that deep into the night.

acknowledgments

This novel, more so than others, is deeply personal – but although I traveled this dark journey, I did so as a supporting character. Infinite thanks to the young man who played the lead and who, when at last we reached the other side, said, "Yes, okay, you can share my story. Maybe it will help someone else along the way." (That said, Paul's story is neither biographical nor autobiographical. I made *all this shit up*. It's classified as fiction for good reason!)

Because the story is so personal, it spilled initially onto the page as a big gory mess, embarrassing and wandering and unformed. Seriously, it was ugly. And then – praise be to friends! Sarah Mlynowski and Emily Lockhart Jenkins both gave the manuscript a careful read and told me how to begin to mold the bloody scraps into something more whole. You ladies are phenomenal; I am forever in your debt.

A handful of doctors and therapists informed my understanding of addiction and recovery, although none of them knew I'd be incorporating their wisdom into a novel. James Kagan, Susie Klingner, John Guenther, Jim Shuler, and Mark Benn: thank you for being so awesome. The stuff I got wrong? That's on me. Anything I got right is thanks to y'all.

When someone in a family goes through rough times, the entire family is impacted. Thanks, family, for remaining stalwart. Special thanks to Susan White and Sam Reid, who said, "Huh. Didn't expect this to land on our doorstep, but ... okay! Come on in, and we will hug you and feed you!" Double-special thanks to Ruth and Tim White, who let me be their daughter at a time when I so desperately needed parenting, so that I could then nod and straighten my spine and go off and parent my own sweet child. Don and Sarah Lee Myracle weren't in the vicinity when this particular drama unfolded, but their love and support helped hold me up as well. (And I went on to set Paul's story in their hometown and my birthplace, Brevard, North Carolina. Dad and Sarah Lee, you're present in every waterfall.)

A different sort of thanks goes to my daughter, Mirabelle, who has gone through *a lot* with both Al *and* Jamie. Mirabelle, you never lost faith in those darling complicated brothers of yours, and the power of your love means more than you know.

Ali Pezeshki! Ha ha! I pronounced it correctly, didn't I? Can't argue with me this time, because it's in print. Ali had dinner with Randy and me during a time when I couldn't for the life of me figure out how to begin *This Boy*. Ali graciously shared his story of watching *A Star Is Born* during its theatrical release, after which he shed manly tears while pissing into a urinal in the men's room. The man standing next to Ali had seen the same movie, and he, too, was silently crying as he took a piss. Ali and the stranger never made eye contact, but a nod of acknowledgment allegedly transpired. "It was the most genuine man-to-man conversation I've ever had," concluded Ali, and voilà, Paul's story had a beginning. Ali, you dignified devil, I adore you.

Thanks to my agent, the incomparable Barry Goldblatt, for caring more about good fiction than about money, even though, yeah-yeah, I know you care about both, and one day you may even persuade me to care about both, too. You take awfully good care of me!

Thank you to my new Candlewick/Walker Books family for ushering this baby into the world with such genius! Karen Lotz, Karen Walsh, Lindsay Warren, Maya Tatsukawa, John Mendelson, Jennifer Roberts, JoAnne Sweeney, Susan Batcheller, Sally Bratcher, Kate Hurley, Maggie Deslaurier, Kim Lanza, Angela Dombroski, Erin DeWitt, Matt Seccombe, and Emily Quill, you sure know how to make an author feel welcome, and you are all amazing at what you do. Maria Middleton, you are the absolute best art director in the multiverse. The cover you designed for *This Boy*! Aaaaah! It is glorious.

As for my longtime editor and dear sweet friend, Susan Van Metre, I just ... I can't even. I'm a writer! I'm supposed to know how to do the "words" thing! But when I think of all you've done for me, for this book, for life and the universe and everything, I turn all gooey and weepy. The good sort of gooey and weepy, obviously, but still, I just ... you know ... yeah. ☺ All right, I'll try: Susan, you make me a better writer and a better human. Your heart, as an editor and a friend, is rivaled by no other. And you're just ~~fucking~~ frickin' brilliant. (Look, I edited myself! For you! That's how much I love you!) You figure out what story I'm trying to tell waaaaay before I do. You are gentle and you are kind, but you are relentless, lady, and you always make me tell that story to the best of my ability. Damn. I kind of like you *a lot*. Have you figured that out yet?

And Randy. My love. You bring me joy in a million different ways – which I will not enumerate here, as some things are best kept private. (Kids? You're welcome.) Thank you for being my darling man and for letting me be your darling woman. As Paul says, we all need each other; but baby, I need you most of all.

about the author

Lauren Myracle is the author of numerous best-selling novels for young adults, including the Internet Girls series (*ttyl*; *ttfn*; *l8r, g8r*; and *yolo*); *Shine*; *The Infinite Moment of Us*; *Under the Moon: A Catwoman Tale*; and *Let It Snow*, which she wrote with John Green and Maureen Johnson and which has been made into a film. She lives with her family in Fort Collins, Colorado.